FRANCIS MARION BEYNON

(1884-1951) was born near Streetsville, Ontario, the second youngest of seven children. Her parents, Rebecca Manning and James Barnes Beynon, were third generation farmers of Scots-Irish descent.

In 1889, when Francis was five years old, they left Ontario and moved to the province of Manitoba to homestead land near the village of Hartney. Here she attended the local school, and trained for a position as a primary school teacher; a role she never fulfilled. Instead, she moved to Winnipeg in 1908 and her first job was in the advertising department of a large store, where she became one of the earliest Canadian women in this profession. By this time Francis' elder sister, Lillian, was a journalist on the Manitoba *Free Press*, and both sisters quickly became preoccupied with writing and public affairs. They were responsible for the foundation of the literary Quill Club, and served on the Winnipeg branch of the Canadian Women's Press Club, also helping to launch the Political Equality League of Manitoba; an organisation dedicated to women's enfranchisement.

In 1912 Francis Marion Beynon assumed direction of the women's page of an agricultural journal, the *Grain Grower's Guide*, where she demonstrated her concern with pacifism and women's rights. With the outbreak of the First World War, however, her strident pacifism became increasingly unpopular, and in 1917, forced out of her job, she moved to New York. *Aleta Dey*, her first and only novel, was published two years later; she subsequently slipped into obscurity, returning to Canada only once, shortly before her death.

D0465713

VIRAGO
MODERN
CLASSIC
NUMBER

288

FRANCIS MARION BEYNON

ALETA
DEY

WITH A NEW INTRODUCTION BY
ANNE HICKS

Published by VIRAGO PRESS Limited 1988
Centro House, 20-23 Mandela Street, London NW1 0HQ.

First published in Great Britain by C. W. Daniel Ltd 1919
Copyright Francis Marion Beynon 1919

Introduction Copyright © Anne Hicks 1988

British Library Cataloguing in Publication Data

A CIP catalogue record for this book is available from the
British Library

Printed in Great Britain by Cox & Wyman of Reading, Berks

INTRODUCTION

How does one "explain" the theme of traumatic marginalisation that underlies this early twentieth-century novel by a feminist and pacifist who was a prominent journalist at the time of the First World War? Perhaps by imagining a street full of busy ants crawling in picnic fascination about the tipped-over marble bust of a woman's head, one can picture the enormous neglect awaiting feminist intellectuals after the War. In a vulgarly realist vein, this novel might be described as the fictionalised autobiography of a fervent suffragist who really wants to climb into a nightie to pursue her passion for a man. While that might occasionally be agreed to at midnight, there are dangerous flaws for women in any conventional and grossly conciliatory romance, as this ambitiously post-Victorian woman sensed. Aleta Dey's personal and (for her time) radical dis-ease with the traditional content of marriage is apparent from adolescence when her socialist school-mate, Ned, complacently aims choking domestic ideology her way. "'What's the use of starting a lot of things and having to give them up when you get married?'" he demands as they sit side by side on the steps of her parents' front verandah. Aleta is deeply hurt by this demeaning attitude, but how was her creator to erect a feminist critique of conventional marriage upon a sloppy, sanctimonious sea of Victorian family ideology in 1918, when this novel was composed?

After encountering Aleta's intelligent scepticism of the

grossly subservient ideals surrounding marriage, readers will be dismayed to discover that her grown-up romantic desire is represented by a domineering and discreditable character named McNair. He is a lover and would-be husband whose political arrogance presents too obvious a contrast to Aleta's humane uncertainty and whose implausibly sentimental portrayal becomes irritating. McNair is less a Conservative than a Tory reactionary in politics, it seems. He is also a cloyingly chivalrous Victorian-style playboy whose emotional repertoire has consisted of a saintly "mom" and an "unfeeling" actress-prostitute as a first wife. Luckily for Aleta, as well as the reader, he also has an adolescent charge, Colin, who nurses a self-pitying McNair through his alcoholic sulks while Aleta attempts to survey some of the social and human corruption that underlies the War and examine her own fragile position as a left of centre political critic in a militarised and increasingly intolerant Canadian society.

A perplexed (and brave) *Times Literary Supplement* reviewer praised this pointedly pacifist and feminist novel in 1919 largely due to its offsetting romanticism.

The genuineness of the story and of Aleta herself (whose opinions never really deepen into fanaticism), her bravery and her trusting love, make a real impression on the reader as the story moves towards its close.

While that manner of assessing a significant work should provoke a snort today, Beynon's development of Aleta was quite craftily disarming. Through a series of bruising childhood rebellions against decaying forms of authority, she carefully grounded her post-Victorian feminist in many of her colleagues and contemporaries own

underlying sympathies. By fashioning her fictional
narrative as attractive autobiography, Francis also
challenged (and undoubtedly angered) those former
acquaintances in Winnipeg's war-divided reform
community who had always viewed her as a dowdy,
bookish and intolerably thorny little upstart of a woman.
Beynon was in pacifist exile in Brooklyn, New York when
she composed *Aleta Dey*. By choosing an autobiographical
style she could expand into critical rhetoric or revert to
ruminative and scolding comments on wartime Canadian
political culture, whilst transfiguring her own emotional
experience of public effacement and enforced public
silence into the fictional life of her clever and darkly
disturbed intellectual. By imaginatively creating Aleta,
this ex-journalist probably also kept from plunging into a
deep and useless despair as militarism maimed,
demoralised or disheartened so many of her own
progressive friends and profited important and respected
public figures in Canada.

Francis Marion Beynon was born 21 May 1884 near
Streetsville, Ontario, the second youngest of the seven
children of Rebecca Manning and James Barnes Beynon.
Of Scots-Irish descent, her parents were third generation
Canadian farmers and staunch Wesleyan Methodists
whose own parents had been pioneer settlers of land
north of Toronto in the counties of York and Simcoe.
Methodist clergymen were second only to the farmers
who crammed the Beynon and Manning genealogies,
the most notable ministers in the family being Rebecca
Manning's three brothers. Together, they gave 134
years of service to the Methodist Church of Canada,
Charles Manning securing the prestigious national post of

General Secretary of Home Missions by the turn of the century.

The harsh, righteous father in *Aleta Dey* who flings passages from Paul at his wife, and the mother who seeks poetry in the Bible and feminine self-esteem in the contemporary church, are character portraits of James and Rebecca. Francis had written about them before, briefly but bitterly, complaining to her newspaper readers in 1914 that her parents' many arguments had undermined her childhood respect for their judgement. This was a curious complaint from such an ambitiously progressive intellectual. But as the child of a dogma-ridden marriage, Francis had undoutbedly felt the impact of her parents collapsing ideals and ambitions quite painfully.

At fifty-four and forty-two respectively, James and Rebecca Beynon decided to try homesteading on the Canadian prairies. The acquisition of land in the new but rapidly developing West represented the last opportunity for Francis's father to become a prosperous man through the tricky combination of farming and land speculation he had always fancied. Francis was just five years old when the Beynons left Ontario in 1889 and took up land in the southwest corner of the province of Manitoba near the village of Hartney. Like many prairie settlers, however, they soon suffered from isolation, harsh winters and inadequate facilities for transporting and marketing their grain. Initially they had to team their wheat twenty miles and Francis was to recall "houses where it was so cold that one ached from the weight of quilts on the bed and the hair felt as if it were freezing to the scalp". It was several miles to the nearest school and her eldest sister, Lillian, who suffered from a tubercular hip, was sent first to relatives in Ontario to attend school and then to the established Manitoba town of Portage La Prairie to complete her training as a teacher. It was a measure of the wilful grandiosity and the bitter failure of their father's Western ambitions that William and Howard, as well as Maude and Francis, trained for poorly paid but secure positions as primary school teachers and that Manning, the eldest son, assumed control of the family's property when Rebecca died of cancer at fifty in 1898.

Between their mother's death and the Beynon's final departure from rural Hartney in 1902, there were three restless and confused years. Manning tried numerous money-making schemes, from acting as a land and insurance agent, to selling farm implements and even bicycles in the district. Lillian, now twenty-four, taught in primary schools in nearby districts, returning to Hartney as often as possible to provide financial as well as emotional and intellectual support to Francis and her brothers and sisters as they each completed the senior school year necessary to qualify. And sixteen-year-old Maude and fourteen-year-old Francis took charge of their younger brother Rueben, who died later, tragically, at fifteen. Their father was known to neighbours and family friends as physically ailing, his manner distracted and erratic and not simply contentious. James must have angrily resisted his children's attempts to move him from the country to Winnipeg in 1902 where he would be cared for (probably by Lillian). He was to die farming a lonely plot of new homestead land near Estevan, Saskatchewan, four years after his children had left the small, isolated community.

Francis's eldest sister, Lillian, immediately set out to build an enviable public career. She enrolled in Wesley College, Winnipeg, where she was influenced by social gospel intellectuals such as Reverend Salem Bland and W. F. Osborne who believed in a dynamic fusion between Christian New Testament ethics and concrete social reform. In 1906, after teaching in a high school for a year, she landed the position of women's editor of the weekly farm supplement of the Manitoba *Free Press*, Western Canada's most powerful daily newspaper. When the adventurous Kate Simpson Hayes left to publicise Western Canada and the Canadian Pacific Railway in Britain, Lillian soon inherited her prestigious role and in 1911 married fellow employee and political reporter, Vernon Thomas.

By the time she was elected first President of the newly formed Manitoba Political Equality League in 1912, Lillian Beynon Thomas was a prominent figure in Winnipeg reform circles. Significantly, the Political Equality League was the first English-speaking women's suffrage organisation in Manitoba that did not have the conservative, prohibitionist Women's Christian Temperance Union as its direct ancestor. And its ideals— more civil, legal and economic power for women—directly challenged a now painfully corrupt Victorian ideology of a domestic sphere of influence for women. With ten journalists among its members, the Manitoba Political Equality League was able to systematically promote women's suffrage in sympathetic newspapers throughout the West. Western Canadian suffragists also benefited from the talents of literary celebrity Nellie McClung whose 1908 novel, *Sowing Seeds in Danny*, was a North American bestseller. McClung's brilliant imitation of the corpulent figure and flattering manner of anti-suffrage premier, Sir Rodmond Roblin, in a League stage production and her speeches against the scandal-ridden Conservatives in two successive provincial elections were notable factors in toppling the Roblin government. In just a matter of months the promised women's suffrage bill would be passed when the Liberals took office in August 1915.

Francis had fervently promoted women's enfranchisement as a journalist on the small but powerful, populist *Grain Growers' Guide*. However, unlike Lillian and Nellie—her intimate colleagues—she was neither an inspiring nor an entertaining public speaker. Francis probably functioned in the League's inner circle as their backroom voice, making clever, deflating observations on some of the prominent people Lillian and Nellie had to coax into League membership or flatter into political support for enfranchisement. Francis's singular contribution occurred in 1916. The newly elected Liberal government of T. C. Norris secretly attempted to add a clause to their promised women's suffrage bill excluding women from running for provincial office. At the time, Francis was reporting on the Annual Meeting of the politically powerful Manitoba Grain Growers Association. She promptly used her well-earned influence with the pro-suffrage women's section of the MGGA to ensure that the main convention would condemn any such exclusion. The threat was relayed to Premier Norris by Lillian. And it worked. The newly elected Liberals angrily scrapped the crippling clause rather than risk irritating the MGGA's male executive. On 28 January 1916, women's right to vote in provincial and

national elections and to hold provincial office passed into
Manitoba law, the first of its kind in Canada.

By now Francis was restless. She had followed Lillian to
Winnipeg in 1908 and worked for the advertising division
of the large T. Eaton department store before being hired
as the first fulltime women's editor of *The Grain Growers
Guide* in 1912. During the four year suffrage campaign
she had garnered admiration as well as gratitude from the
numerous women in Western Canada and Ontario who
read her page in *The Guide*. "The Country Homemakers"
as it was called, was a curious, clever mixture of light
entertainment, cultural and literary criticism, opinion
from its female readers on important social issues of the
day, fashions, recipes, social gospel reform politics and
exposure of the most pressing inequities facing farm
women. The most glaring of these was the absence of
property rights for married women, an issue Francis
regularly raised. She also produced a host of "practical"
routine details from the daily working lives of Manitoba's
farm women to constantly insinuate the enormous
economic contribution rural women made to the capital
value as well as to the maintenance of the family farm.
This was, in part, her fierce, loving tribute to her mother,
now dead for over a decade. But it was a *memento mori*
too. Francis was deeply influenced by Olive Schreiner's
Women and Labour (1911), a dramatic, panoramic
account of the erosion of traditional homemaking skills
and their appropriation by commercial industries. If the
bakery, cannery and clothing manufacturer were rapidly
invading the urban middle-class household, women must
now seek satisfying paid employment. Francis often
mentioned *Woman and Labour* to her readers. It

certainly contained an analysis she prescribed for herself and one she used to distinguish her own life from her mother's.

At thirty-one, Francis was a well-known journalist in English Canada and a notable intellectual. Her fear of the increasing war fever in English Canada surfaced in *The Guide* in March 1915, in her report on the formation of a Women's Peace Party in the United States. When she seriously turned her attention to the War later that year, she had a large and loyal readership and almost complete editorial control over the "women's content" in *The Guide*. The dramatic consequences of Francis Beynon's incisive and persistent criticisms of militarism, xenophobia and the Canadian military establishment in her columns can be found in Wendy Lill's moving play *The Fighting Days*. Two events best characterise the importance and the painful cost of Beynon's pacifism. The first was her angry public disagreement with her prominent former suffragist friend, Nellie McClung, who, in a private, patriotic audience with Prime Minister Borden, reassured him that he should disenfranchise all Canadian women who were "aliens"—in other words, women who had been born in Eastern Europe. The second, was Francis's forced resignation as women's editor of *The Guide* in June 1917 due to her public opposition to male conscription. The tapping of Aleta's phone by an agent of the Canadian Press Censor is probably biographical fact. The new War Measures Act gave federal government authorities sweeping powers over press communication about the War and the right to fine or imprison violators. By the time of the 1917 conscription crisis, Canada's chief press censor, Colonel

Ernest Chambers, had assembled a shrewd and aggressive cadre of "gentlemanly" censors. At least one small newspaper had been suspended for three months in the previous year for openly opposing the War. In July 1917, now deeply shaken, Francis took a train from Winnipeg to Brooklyn, New York. Lillian and Vernon were already there, their careers on the *Free Press* also casualties of Canadian war fever. Lillian had produced several approving statements concerning pacifism in her *Free Press* column. When her husband publicly shook hands with politician Fred Dixon after Dixon spoke out against conscription in the Manitoba Legislature, the *Free Press* editor, John W. Dafoe, swiftly fired him.

The last quarter of *Aleta Dey* contains Beynon's sickened sense of grief and anger over the militarism that had swept through Canadian society and politics. And it is in this portion that the novel's mood splits and swings like a pendulum, from peculiar, nihilistic despair to the archaic romanticism of its conclusion. Why? McNair, I think.

In constructing this character, Francis was attempting to pay tribute to a man she loved who died in the slaughter of 1916. As poignant and important as that emotional tribute may have been, it was certainly a literary failure. The explanation resides in the underside of late-Victorian patriarchy. An era that could produce Freud had ruthlessly suppressed women and McNair is an infantilised, capitalist double of the Calvinist God with which James Barnes Beynon had so ruthlessly suppressed Francis's mother.

Francis Beynon was terribly sceptical of early twentieth-century notions of political change, yet she tried to hold on to late-Victorian theories of radical historical progress. McNair is, understandably, a reactionary private fantasy, but he also functions as political allegory. Canada's late-Victorian conservatism was intellectually and emotionally senile, like McNair, and the political socialism represented by the fictional American lawyer, Ned Grant, was slick and over-confident. But both possessed social, cultural and economic force.

Francis remained in New York City after the War, a writer and intellectual in both emotional and physical exile. In the heady "jazz age" of American capitalism, suffragists were just artifacts and any woman who insisted that she had an impressive intellect was largely a giggle. Although Francis's social milieu was intellectually different from that of present-day Canadian feminists, I find her voice quite haunting. *Aleta Dey* stands not only as a curious reminder of how destructive Victorian patriarchy was for women, but also as a poignant personal testimony against war.

Anne Hicks, Ontario, 1987

PREFACE

Though the winds of popular caprice are almost as variable as those of nature it did not seem possible back in the dark days of military tyranny, when this book was written, that the day would come in the lifetime of any radical then living, when the tables would be turned over a large portion of a great continent.

But so it is to-day, and with the radicals in the saddle in several European countries, we see the sorry spectacle of history repeating itself and the oppressed becoming the oppressor. My mind refuses to make any distinction between the tyranny of radicals and the tyranny of conservatives. As I see it, tyranny wears many wigs, but he has only one complexion.

It is neither excuse nor palliation of this tendency to suppress conservative opinion to say that they are only getting their own back. Revenge is the meagre dream of little minds. It is like the remembered table delights of our childhood, which when repeated in maturity are flat and unpalatable.

Perhaps if the conservative mind would

show that it had learned anything from this great upheaval the situation would be somewhat relieved. But regrettably it does not. It has not even sufficient honesty to face the fact that the anarchy it hates is the logical conclusion of the war which it loved.

The militarist felt that he had the pacifist in a difficult position when he asked him if he would stand by and see his mother murdered. And he had. It would have been conclusive were it not that the militarist was not one whit less willing to face the logical conclusion of war—which is that it is our duty to murder anyone whose conduct and opinions seem to us to be injurious to the state in which we live—that, indeed, we need only notify the Almighty that he is on our side to make it a religious obligation.

The New York alderman who said he would not hesitate to murder traitors to the flag was at least partially consistent; to be fully so he would have to admit that it was the duty of any other citizen, who felt his opinions were injurious, to murder him. Likely as not he would boggle at that.

And that is anarchy, if you please.

But as I did not believe in war, and the anarchistic methods of war governments, neither do I believe in revolution and the oppressive measures of revolutionary governments. It is not possible for any group of people in a country either to inspire or to feel the emotion of fear without spiritually degrading the whole. So it is imperative that the most rampant militarist, imperialist and royalist be protected in the right of every man to think his honest thoughts aloud, even if to insure this some of us, whom in their day of power they so ruthlessly suppressed have once again to take up the heavy burden of rowing against the tide of public opinion, sweeping along as furiously as before in the narrow channels of bigotry.

But only so can we ourselves be free, for whether we like it or not, our spirits are chained to the most craven in the country and the limitation of their dreams contracts our own horizon.

THE AUTHOR.

CONTENTS.

CHAPTER I.

A COWARD.

I am a coward.

I think I was born to be free, but my parents, with God as one of their chief instruments of terror, frightened me into servility. Perhaps I owe it to the far horizons of my Canadian prairie birth-place; perhaps to the furious tempests that rocked our slim wooden dwelling, or it may be to the untrammelled migration of birds to distant lands that the shame of being a coward has survived their chastening. I know that these things have always beckoned to something in me that vainly beat its wings against the bars of life.

Mother and father began when Jean and I were barely out of the cradle to perform a task called "breaking our spirit," which seemed to them essential to our well-being. My mother did it reluctantly, from a stern sense of Christian duty, but my father seemed to take a solid satisfaction in the work. Between them they succeeded so well that now when my employer rings for me my first sensation is always fear.

It is wonderful how early one can be made
into a coward. I was one at five. I remember
a golden summer morning when the milk pans
were all about the kitchen and the flies were
buzzing back and forth between them and the
window. Jean was tugging at my hair and I
slapped her hands and said, " Darn you, stop
that."

Mother's portly figure revolved until she
was facing me.

" What did you say, Aleta? " she demanded
sharply.

" Nothing," I answered, looking down at
my copper-toed shoes.

" She said ' Darn you,' " Jean put in, with
a self-righteous smirk.

Mother picked me up; set me in my high
chair and promised to whip me at noon.

It was a long, long morning, and I spent
most of it in bitter plans for revenge. If
mother were one of those flies I'd stamp on
her and squash her into nothing. I'd run
away and drown myself in the big pond and
then she'd be sorry, and I'd be glad if she
was. So I thought and thought as I boiled
internally with childish rage and impotence.

After a long time she took a strap down
from a nail behind the door. All at once I

ceased to be angry and became afraid. I did
not want to be struck. Mother came over and
set me down on the floor. I thought she
looked very ugly as she stood over me with
the strap in her hands.

" Hold out your right hand," she commanded. I hesitated. I did not want to, but
I could see that she meant to strike me some-
where, so I held it out. She brought the
strap down on it smartly twice, and I
whimpered.

" Now the left."

She slapped that twice.

" Are you sorry you said darn? " she inquired in a threatening voice.

I thought a moment and found I was not,
so I said nothing.

" You must not get stubborn," she insisted,
and began slapping me harder and faster, and
the harder she slapped, the less sorry I felt.

But she was determined to have the lie, so
at last, when my hands were all red and
stinging and I was choking with sobs, I whispered between catches in my breath, " I'm
sorry," and she stopped. God knows I
wouldn't have done it only I was so very
little and it was the only way to stop her.

But I was ashamed to meet the big wind

when I went out to play, and I tried to show
him I was not a coward by shaking my little
fist at the house and shouting, " I'm not
sorry, and I hate you—I hate you—I hate
you."

I was not at all sure that I deceived the
wind. I suspected that he knew all the time
that I was a coward.

Having learned physical fear so young it is
no wonder that I lacked the courage to com-
mit suicide on the morning of my christening,
which happened that autumn. Through a
peculiar set of circumstances, long since forgotten, I had missed being christened in my
infancy, so it was arranged that the Rev.
Foster Forsyth, the Methodist minister, should
come out on a certain day and rectify the
omission.

" He'll set you in the middle of the room
and turn a bucket of water over you,"
declared Letty, our hired girl.

I was aghast and ran to mother to ask about
it. She was not a cruel woman, and usually
she did not allow us to be frightened, but I
think she did not understand my alarm and
mortification in this case. She just laughed
and said nothing, either way.

I met our hired man John coming in from

the barn and asked him about it, and he, too, laughed and said a bath would do me good.

John was a remittance man. In the beginning England sent her younger sons of great families to Canada, and her criminals to Australia, and judging by some of the results our cousin had an unfair advantage over us.

How we born Canadians detested those English remittance men! Mr. A. G. Gardiner mentions in one of his books the days when it was not disrespectful to speak of "the colonies," and by the tone of his remarks one feels that he cannot understand the resentment felt by the overseas dominions at the use of the expression.

If Mr. Gardiner could have heard John say to my father, as I did, " You colonials, what do you know? " he would begin to comprehend.

My father combed the chaff out of his beard and answered, " Well, my man, I know how to plough a straight furrow."

" And that is about all you do know," John retorted contemptuously.

It was not quite fair. My father was not an educated man in the Englishman's sense of the word, but he took a deep interest in politics and kept himself well informed on the questions of the day. Moreover, we Canadians had a theory that it was a breach of the law of courtesy to tell people so bluntly of their shortcomings, and of the law of democracy to set oneself up as a judge of one's fellow men. When help became more plentiful our advertisements, like those of most of our neighbours, used to read, " No Englishman need apply."

I am sorry for those English remittance men now, at a distance of years from contact with them. Our crude way of living must have been as distasteful to them as their avowed contempt for everything we did, thought and had was to us.

But I was too young then to philosophise, and John's heartless laugh at my childish anxiety over my christening was, very unjustly, chalked up in my child mind against England.

I cannot explain the horror I felt at the thought of the public humiliation that had to be faced on the day of my christening. As the time approached my terror grew. On the night before it was to happen I found sleep impossible. I felt I could not lie awake in the dark and think of it, so I poked Jean in the side

"Jean, Jean," I whispered.

Jean shut her mouth, turned her fair head
the other way about on the pillow; opened
her mouth and began to snore.

"Jean," I insisted, shaking her resolutely.

She opened her blue eyes and looked at me
dreamily, "Is it morning?" she asked.

"Shssh!" I whispered. "It isn't morning."

"Then what for did you waken me?"

I slipped my arm about her neck. "Jean,
do you think they'll pour a bucket of water
over me to-morrow?"

"Letty said they would," she confirmed
my terror.

I began to cry and Jean sat up in bed and
put her arms around me in a motherly fashion,
for she was a year my senior.

"Don't cry, Aleta," she begged, "don't
cry. Maybe it won't hurt much."

There was poor comfort in that and I wept
more and more bitterly.

Presently Jean slipped out of bed and
fumbled about the bureau. When she came
back she pressed her string of amber beads
into my hand.

"You can have my beads if you won't cry,"

she promised. I slipped them under my pillow and we fell asleep locked in each other's arms.

But I wakened with the consciousness of impending disaster, which in its fullest detail rushed back into my mind. I was going to be christened to-day.

As I have said I cannot explain the horror I felt at the prospect of being set in the midst of a roomful of adults and having a bucket of water poured over me. I was sure I could never be happy again if it happened.

After breakfast I stole away by myself to the big pond. The heavy dew on the grass made my feet sopping wet, as I went out alone to die. I had fully made up my mind to jump into the pond, but when I came to the edge and looked down I was afraid. The water looked cold and dirty. I did not want to die, especially when mother was making lemon pies for dinner. But I could not bear the thought of what was to happen after dinner.

I stopped beside a scrubby little bush we children called the snowberry, the fruit of which was reputed to be poisonous. We had been warned repeatedly that if we ate those berries we should die. Here was an easier way out than by jumping into the dirty slimy pond. I gathered a handful of the berries. They were little silvery grey white things, which looked harmless enough, and I shoved the whole handful into my mouth.

Then I became afraid. I spat them out upon the ground and ran as fast as I could to the house for a cup of water, which I took out behind the gooseberry bushes and used to rinse my mouth. All the rest of the day I spent listening for trouble internally, so that the dread of the approaching christening became secondary.

When it was over I said to Jean, " Huh, you thought the preacher was going to pour a bucket of water over my head."

This was too much for Jean's patience. " You thought so, too," she insisted, " and you were awful scared." " I wasn't scared," I contradicted her flatly.

We were playing in the sand-pile with Minnie Forsyth and Amy Cotter, whose mothers had brought them along to my christening. Minnie created a diversion at this juncture by announcing, " I heard my ma tell my pa your mother is going to have a baby."

Jean and I gasped.

" I know, the stork brings them," Amy explained.

Minnie sat back on her heels after having rounded off a mud pie, and said contemptuously, " Silly, that's not the way babies come." And there, while we knelt open-mouthed around her in the sand-pile, she explained to us, with illustrations drawn from the farmyard, the main facts of procreation.

That night when mother was putting me to bed I asked abruptly, " Mother, where do babies come from? "

" The stork brings them," she answered, giving me a quick suspicious look.

" And where does the stork get them? " I persisted, in order to see if she would keep on lying.

Mother blushed. " In heaven," she snapped. " Don't ask so many questions."

I looked at mother's figure thoughtfully. I did not so much mind being a liar, now that I knew mother was one too. I wondered if God would let her go to heaven when she died. I hoped so, for I loved mother.

CHAPTER II.

Baby Brother.

It was winter. The snow was piled higher than my head, in places higher than my father's also, along the garden fence, and the windows were thick with frost. Mother used to take a flat iron from the stove and thaw them off, because it made the room dark. We slept with such heavy coverings on our bed that we wakened tired with the weight of them, and gathering up our clothes ran down to the kitchen stove to dress.

One day of that winter stands out alone in my memory. It was so cold that the kitchen door creaked ominously on its hinges when father went in or out to his chores. He was alone now, for John had gone to the town to work during the winter.

Mother went often to the window and looked out. She moved slowly, as if she were very tired. Once I tagged along and climbed up on a chair and looked out too. There was nothing to see but the snow drifting in big, loose white waves for miles upon miles, to where the level white fields met the blue rim of the sky.

Mother put her arm about me; drew me close to her side, and ran her cracked fingers through my curly red brown hair.

" If mother should have to go away and leave Aleta she would be a good girl, wouldn't she? " she asked.

I put my arms about her neck and clung there desperately " I'll tell God not to let you go away," I remonstrated.

" Do you think it will be to-day? " Letty asked, from the table, where she was making cookies.

" I don't know," mother answered, and sighed a long weary shuddering sigh. " I hope not. It would be a terrible day for Jack to go for the doctor."

When she spoke again her voice was sharp and irritable. " Letty, do take that pot of feed off the stove. The smell of it makes me sick."

Jean and I were sewing for our dolls over in a corner, but when mother went to the window again, an hour or two later, I put down the doll's frock and followed her.

All was changed outside. The sky had grown dark and the snow drifted past in solid white sheets, so that one could not see even the garden fence.

" You can't go away," I said jubilantly,
" look how it storms."

Mother raised my little brown hand to her
lips and kissed it. " One would think she
knew something was the matter," she murmured.

When I came back Jean said, " Why don't
you sit still and sew? "

" I hate sewing," I answered.

" You're lazy," she said.

Perhaps she was right.

*　　*　　*　　*　　*

It was the middle of the night when I was
wakened by a loud cry. I sat up in bed shaking. The cry came again—a fearful agonized
sound. I do not know how I knew it was my
mother crying. The screams died away into a
sob that was even more unbearable to listen
to.

I slipped out of bed and trotted into the
hall in my bare feet. Letty was just coming
out of mother's room.

" Go back to bed right away, Aleta," she
commanded me sharply.

" I want my mother," I whimpered.

" God help you, child; I'm afraid your
mother is dying and your father is lost in the
storm."

"Where's father?" I asked.

"Gone for the doctor. Run back to bed quickly."

I pretended to start for my room, but when she had gone on downstairs with the kettle I tip-toed back and shoved mother's door open a crack. I looked just once. I did not want to look any more. I ran back to bed, where I shivered and sobbed so hard I wakened Jean.

She started up in a fright. "What's the matter?" she asked anxiously.

"Mother's dying and father's lost. Letty says so."

I tried three times to tell her of what I had seen in mother's room, but could not. This is the first time in all these years that I have been able to speak of it.

Jean began to cry too, and I sobbed out, "Mother, mother, mother!" over and over again. Sometimes we both held our breath there in the dark and listened to the wind howling around the house and rattling the window panes.

I don't know which of us fell asleep first, but our next consciousness was that it was morning and the sun was streaming in through our window. Nobody had come to waken us.

Then we remembered about father and mother and got out of bed crying to ourselves; gathered our clothes together and started for the stairs.

As we passed mother's door her voice called out to us, "Girls, come here."

Jean rushed in, but I was afraid to go.

" Come, Aleta," mother called again, and I went shyly in. She was lying in a nice clean bed, and on the pillow beside her there was a wee head.

" Kiss your baby brother," mother suggested.

I did and it made me feel very queer. " Let me hold him," I begged.

" You're too small yet," mother said. " You'll have more than you want of holding him," she added, with her dry cynicism.

She was wrong in that. I think if Barry could be questioned he would agree that her prophecy was never fulfilled.

A big strange man came into the room then, and we remembered about father. Mother told us he had reached home safely and sent us out of the room.

We went downstairs, and shortly afterwards father came in from the stable. He was a tall,

stocky man with bushy whiskers. This morning he wore an air of great importance. He
went round about to kick several chairs and
Rover out of his way.

CHAPTER III.

GOD IN THE STORM.

The following summer they sent me to Sunday School, but that did not improve my opinion of God. The being I heard about there was always angry at somebody about something, and I was afraid of him. There are good people who claim to have met the God of the big quiet places and the starry heavens in churches, but personally I never have. The God I met there wore an expression which I have since seen on the faces of stage policemen applying the third degree to a criminal.

But I met him one afternoon the summer I was nine, in a corner of the pasture field. Mother and father had gone to town, and while Jean sewed a rip in Barry's shirt I went out in the strange brooding hush before a thunderstorm to find the cows.

From the blue black sky, resting evenly, like a bowl, upon the level floor of earth, filtered a weird shadowy twilight, and I looked east and west and north and south, and there was nothing but a few shacks between me and the far away edge of the world. I felt very tiny under that immense black dome, and I was glad even of the barbed wire fence which shut me in from those immeasurable distances.

The bluebells hung tense on their slender stems, and the last whisper had died away among the stunted poplar scrub. Over in the east a yellow snake of fire wriggled down the sky, followed by a crash that seemed to rock the world. A breeze came by. It stirred my hair, ran along the grass at my feet and set all the lilies and bluebells to nodding. Then all was still again and dark, but I felt as if I were riding on the wings of a bird. I know God passed by in that breeze, because for a little while I was not afraid of father or mother, or of anything in the whole world.

But perhaps that is not quite true, for I do not believe I would have had the courage to write in a composition at school any of the strange new things I thought as I drove the cattle home in that queer dark hush before the storm.

The next thing the world must evolve is protective coloration for souls, so that society and our public schools will not be able to pounce upon and trample into the mire of conventionality all the hopeful little buds of inspiration which spring up in children's minds.

CHAPTER IV.

LIGHTNING.

As I neared the house Jean came running to meet me. Her face was as white as chalk, and tears streamed down her cheeks.

"The house has been struck by lightning," she wailed, "and—and I think—its killed Barry."

Everything that happened after that is like a dream. I vaguely remember running like the wind, with Jean panting beside me. I hardly glanced at the torn and blackened wall, but ran straight to the couch where Jean had dragged his limp little body. He was absolutely still. The little hand, with the dimpled knuckles hung over the side of the couch; the fair head was twisted awkwardly to one side.

I caught him in my arms and almost shook him as I cried, "Barry, Barry, waken up quick. Leta wants you."

The small limp figure lay quiet against my shoulder. He did not put the fat little arms about my neck and whisper, as usual, "Barry loves Leta."

Child though I was I can remember yet the

sick thought that he would never do that again; that I would never waken up to find him sitting on my chest or poking his little fingers into my eyes and saying, " I sought you'd never waken up."

" Do you think he's dead? " Jean whispered.

I could not speak, so I just nodded over Barry's little fair head.

" I saw Mary White when she fainted at the Sunday School picnic," Jean said, and they threw cold water on her face, and she got all right."

I put Barry down, and we both ran for the water pail. It was empty, but we took hold of the handle together and ran to the well. It was very dark now, and long wicked chains of lightning ran about the sky at intervals of seconds, while a white light played without intermission along the horizon, and the thunder grumbled continuously, breaking out occasionally into loud crashes. The chip-strewn yard, littered with farm machinery and hen coops, was lighted by a fitful glare. I noticed that all the fowls and animals had crowded into shelter.

Sobbing with terror of the thing that had happened to Barry and of the storm, we

pumped and pumped until we had filled the
pail, and then dragged it between us to the
house, splashing the water over our slippers
and little print skirts.

With shaking hands Jean filled the dipper
and carried it to the couch. Barry was lying
just as we had left him.

"Would you throw it all over him?" she
whispered anxiously.

"I don't know," I said; "what did they do
to Mary?"

"I just forget," she answered, "but I think
they threw a lot." Whereupon she turned the
whole contents of the dipper over Barry's face.

He lay as still as before.

I snatched the dipper and brought it full
again and dashed it over him.

The limp little figure continued motionless,
so I ran frantically for a third. Before I
reached the bench, Jean gave a cry, the inflection of which stays with me to this moment.
When I reached the couch Barry's head was
stirring on the pillow. Jean and I rubbed his
hands and called to him, and presently he
opened his dark blue eyes and began to cry.

We took him up out of the water, and Jean
ran to get dry clothes to put on him. We
were too much excited to think of the storm,

which was roaring and threshing about our prairie dwelling.

By the time we had Barry undressed and into clean clothes the storm had passed. When he stood up on my lap and buried his damp fair head in the hollow of my neck I looked through the open door at the clean, newly-washed world, twinkling and laughing in the sunlight. I laughed, too, but that night I had dreams of losing Barry, and wakened over and over to clutch his warm little body.

CHAPTER V.

School in Town.

We moved, I think it was the following spring, to a farm on the outskirts of a little village called Souris River. Jean and I were allowed to go on ahead with the first load of furniture on a pledge of good behaviour until mother arrived. We pranced up and down and promised anything she asked.

The roads were so bad that the wagon crept along, but the ploughed fields, freshly cleared of snow, were fragrant under the mid-March sun, and we were adventuring forth into a new life.

Always I have loved the up grade of the year, the thrill of a new awakening, even though it is at this season more than any other that I am conscious of that something within which struggles hopelessly to break the bonds of life and find its way to freedom.

The new home seemed to me quite wonderful. The house was big, very big, I thought, for it had a front hall, and there was an archway between the parlour and dining room, and there was a big sunny L of a kitchen. I

was particularly elated over the archway, for
it was just like Minnie Forsyth's and other
places in town, and already I had begun to
accept the world's dictum that the usual is
necessarily the beautiful.

Jean and I were sitting out on the front
steps a week or two later when two little girls
passed, staring very hard at us. We stared
back at them. When they reached the end of
the fence they turned about and marched up
to the gate.

"How much is your gape seed a pound?"
they inquired simultaneously. Then they
took to their heels and ran as fast as they
could towards town. We put down our dolls
and ran after them.

When they reached the culvert over the
ravine they halted, and stood digging the toes
of their shoes into the loose black soil of the
country road.

"What did you say that for?" Jean asked,
when we had come within speaking distance.

The older girl laughed amiably. "Just for
fun," she answered. "What's your name?"

We exchanged names and ages and found
that the strangers were May and Pauline Ransome, and that the former was a year older

than Jean, and Pauline a year older than myself. Their father was a doctor, and they were
Presbyterians. This last was a great blow, as
it eliminated all hope of meeting them at Sunday School. It also, though this worried us
little, put aside any chance of encountering
them in heaven, for already I understood
vaguely that Presbyterians, leaning on the
false prop of fore-ordination, were heading
straight for the burning fiery furnace.

" What grade are you in at school? " May
asked.

Jean and I looked at each other uncomfort-
ably. " We've only been to school two
winters," Jean answered shyly.

The strangers made no attempt to conceal
their amazement.

" You'll have to go in the baby class," May
said, " and everybody will laugh at you. I
wouldn't be in your place for anything."

I could feel my lip tremble as I thought of
the unpleasantness ahead. Then Pauline
leaned over and planted a kiss upon my forehead.

" May and I won't laugh," she promised,
" and you'll soon get ahead."

Jean's face lighted up at that. " Oh, yes,"

she said, easily, " we're very bright and we'll
soon catch up."

For my part I just squeezed Pauline's hand
very hard and said nothing, but I was greatly
comforted. I had found a friend.

And I needed one. I have never forgotten
the unpleasantness of those first few months
at school. It was not being behind girls of my
own age that made me unhappy, for my more
mature mind made promotion come easily,
but being hedged about by a wall of unrelated
don'ts.

One morning after the teacher had read a
chapter from the Bible I put up my hand and
was permitted to speak. " How did God
learn to use such beautiful words? " I asked,
accepting the Bible literally as the word of
God. I can see that room to this day. The
sunlight filtering in through the scrawny
geraniums on the window sill lit up the rows
of still little figures. I can hear yet the hush
that followed my question.

Then the teacher laughed and the children
tittered. Already the public school had
taught us to titter when authority laughs,
which is one of its great functions in society.

" That is a very foolish question, Aleta,"

the teacher said, dismissing it, and my fellow
students looked at me pityingly. I glanced
across at Pauline. She was not laughing, but
she looked shocked and troubled.

" Attention ! "　the　teacher　exclaimed,
sharply.

We turned our heads straight to the front
and put our feet evenly on the floor.

" Books out; one, two, three."

In three exactly uniform movements we
placed our hands on each side of our exercise
books, drew them towards us and slid them
on to the desk. The day had begun.

All morning I worked away with an under-
current of resentment that my wonder at the
compelling beauty of the Biblical language
should have been turned into an occasion for
derision.

I cannot remember the time when the melodious measures of the old Hebrew poets did
not delight my ear, although I understood
only a sentence or two here and there.

When father was away from home mother
used to read for prayers, always selecting some
of those especially lilting passages from the
Psalms, Isaiah or Ecclesiastes, particularly
from the latter that magnificent picturesque

chapter beginning, " Remember now thy
Creator in the days of thy youth . . . ."

Father's favourite passages were : " Honour
thy father and thy mother," and " Wives submit yourselves unto your own husbands." He
never failed to read this advice of Paul's when
he and mother had had a quarrel.

CHAPTER VI.

PUNISHMENT.

There was a big boy in Pauline's class called
Ned Grant, whom I liked. He never laughed
at me for what the rest called my queer questions, which popped out sometimes in spite of
myself, though at longer and longer intervals.

Ned Grant's father was an American
Socialist and agnostic, who, after losing his
wife, had come west and taken a farm adjoin-
ing the one to which we moved.

Theoretically mother did not approve of
him, but she enjoyed his conversation more
than that of most of her neighbours, and she
mended for him and his son, and made their
bread. Her practical tolerance so far outran
her theories of conduct that in spite of her
narrow code of morality she counted her
friends among all classes and sects.

So partly on account of my mother's kindness; partly because of his own radical up-
bringing, I could always count on Ned's support. I needed it less and less, however, as I
learned through a long process of humiliation
that one may ask questions at school about

arithmetic, spelling, geography, and the dates
of history, but one must not inquire and it is
immoral to think about the genesis of life,
God, except in certain set phrases, or the
spirit of history.

Minnie Forsyth, who is now a missionary to
the poor long suffering Chinese, had a knack
of always asking the right kind of question. I
recollect that she looked up in the teacher's
face one day and asked sweetly, " Please,
teacher, does God love me? "

The teacher answered sanctimoniously,
" Yes, dear, God loves everyone : only of
course there are some who are naughty and
have to be punished," she added quickly, as if
God's unmeasured love might be too great a
licence to happiness.

Minnie responded properly, " Thank you,
teacher dear."

The Psalmist exclaimed in apparent surprise, " Why do the heathen rage? " I know
one reason.

I, on the contrary, always asked the for-
bidden thing. Our teacher read a chapter one
morning in which one of the prophets, in the
name of the Lord, threatened a tribe with
complete annihilation at the outset, and at the

end assured them that the Lord had turned
away his wrath from them.

When she had finished I inquired in all sincerity, " Teacher " (I could never be brought
to use that servile form of address, " Please,
teacher "), " does God often change His
mind? "

She looked " the lake that burneth forever"
at me. Immediately the class, taking its cue
from her, fixed its eyes upon me with a "poor
lost soul " expression.

" Aleta, you are a very irreverent little
girl," she said, in a voice of awful solemnity.
" God doesn't love little girls who are
irreverent."

Then she adjusted her spectacles over her
pale blue eyes and went on with her work. I
felt a poke at my elbow, and the girl behind
handed me a note. It was from Ned Grant.
He said, " You're a brick, Aleta."

That evening Pauline, May and Ned walked
home with Jean and me. It was a perfect
June day. The sky was so brilliant one could
not bear to look up at it, and the flower-dotted
grass along the road allowance made a lovely
fresco for the dark billowy fields of grain.

Much to my discomfort Ned deliberately

brought up the question I had asked in the morning.

"Miss Black thinks she knows all about God and the Bible, doesn't she?" he asked.

"Well, I think Aleta's question was sort of disrespectful," Pauline said. "I don't think you should ask questions like that about God." She swung along the dusty road decisively, a sombre, black-haired, dark-eyed, long-limbed girl.

"Why not?" Ned inquired. His voice was contemptuous, for there had long been a mutual dislike between him and Pauline.

"Because it's wrong."

"How do you know it is?" Ned persisted.

Pauline flushed angrily, and was about to speak when May, who was in the room above ours, interrupted, "What are you talking about?" she questioned.

When she was told she disposed of the matter in a sentence. "The teacher ought to have spanked you, Aleta."

"No, she oughtn't," said Jean. Then she changed the subject.

Barry came running out to meet us. "Mother's making lemon tarts," he called, "and she said you could bring Pauline and Ned and May in to have some."

He named our guests in the order of his
own preference. Already he was standing in
the circle of Pauline's arms, giving her a
" love."

" You're Pauline's boy, aren't you? " she
asked.

" I'm Leta's boy first, then Jean's and then
Pauline's," he answered.

We walked on, Pauline and I, each holding
a moist, dirty little hand, except when Barry
withdrew it to tuck the bottom of his blue
duck blouse inside his little pants.

After the tarts we went out to play about the
barn. This was always a treat to the village
children, and we, who were poor and had so
few things to show off with, were rather proud
to have this advantage over them.

We were climbing up and sliding down a
haystack when father came along. He had
been very sullen since morning, when a man
had come to see him about a mortgage. Now
he flew into a terrible rage.

" What are you children doing there? " he
roared.

We scrambled out of the haystack and stood
before him, our hair and dresses full of straw.

" Who told you to bring these youngsters

here? " he demanded, his eyes turning from Jean to me.

" Mother said we might," Jean answered, meekly.

" Your mother ought to know better then," he retorted fiercely. " Go on home with you," he continued, turning to our guests. " I'm not going to have a lot of kids tearing my haystack to pieces."

They went. And we stood trembling with rage and fear before him. I cannot express the bitter humiliation of having our guests dismissed in this way.

" I'll teach you," he raged; " I'll teach you to bring a lot of youngsters around here to destroy things."

He went around the corner of the barn and came back in a moment with a stick.

" Hold out your hand," he said to Jean. She did, and he made six dark welts on it with the stick. Jean screamed.

" Now the other one."

His fury and brutality were rising, and he brought the blood on this hand. Jean's screams were terrible, and Barry ran wailing to the house.

I was sick with fear at the sight of this human creature, mad with the lust for physical

conquest over anything that stood in his way.
Had I been brave I would have defied him,
but I was very little and terribly afraid. So I
ran as fast as I could and crawled into a hole
in the haystack. I did not know then that
one should never run from an infuriated
animal unless one is sure one can run faster.

Father ran after me and dragged me out by
the foot. He was pale, and his face was working horribly. He did not wait to ask that I
hold out my hand, but struck me furiously and
indiscriminately with the stick.

" Are you sorry you've been a bad girl? "
he kept demanding hoarsely, between blows.

Sorry ! The one thought in my mind at
that moment was murder. There is no more
horrible spectacle than that of a human being
drunk with the desire for victory over the
body of another human being. The revolting
thing is that in reverting himself to the emotions of the jungle he drags his victim down
with him to the level of a beast of prey. We,
the attacker and the attacked, were for the
time being on the spiritual plane of the tiger
and the ape.

" Are you sorry? " he roared.

Still I said nothing. I was too much of a
coward to defy him, but he had overdone the

brutality, and even my craven heart was roused to a passive resistance.

I screamed at the top of my voice, and presently mother came from the house and said, " Jack, you must stop whipping that child."

" You go away and mind your business," father snapped, but in a wavering voice.

Mother came up and looked him straight in the eye. Then she took the stick from him and threw it as far as she could throw. I remember how her tight black alpaca waist slipped up away from her skirt, as she raised her plump brown arm, on which the sleeve was rolled up to the elbow. She was a little roly poly woman with plain features, of which mine are a duplicate, but at that moment she was magnificent. A soul had come into the jungle.

Jean and I had been wrought up to such a pitch of nervous excitement that we sobbed short, dry sobs all the evening, and lay staring into the dark long after we had finished our lessons and gone to bed.

Suddenly there flashed into my mind a picture of father getting down on his knees after supper, as he always did, and praying. I saw him very vividly, with a hand on each side of a well-scrubbed kitchen chair, and his beard

tilted towards the ceiling, as he thanked God
for keeping him from sin during the day.

"Did you hear him praying to God?" I
whispered to Jean.

"And after he'd been such a pig," Jean
agreed.

"If he goes to heaven I don't want to; I'd
rather go to hell," I exclaimed, growing more
reckless, and yet secretly hoping that the devil
wasn't listening, and would not take too
prompt an advantage of my preference.

Barry sat up in his cot and looked about
him. Then there was a patter of little bare
feet on the floor, as he climbed up and cuddled
his warm little body against mine.

"Never mind, Leta," he whispered; "when
I'm a man I'll get a gun and shoot him dead,
so I will."

"No, Barry dear, you can't do that," I
whispered back regretfully, "because they
would put you in jail or hang you."

"What are you children talking about?"
father's voice asked sharply from the door,
where he had come to spy upon us. It was a
peculiarity of his that he wanted the sensual
satisfaction of a physical victory together with
the respect which belongs to a spiritual one.

CHAPTER VII.

THE SPIRITUAL X-RAY.

From around the corner of the barn one evening in my twelfth summer Jean and I saw Mr. Elton, the Methodist minister, drive into the yard. We watched mother come out to speak to him, rolling down her sleeves as she came; watched him get down from the seat and begin to unhitch his long-haired bay horse from the shabbily respectable buggy, which so well matched his dingy black ministerial coat. Then we effaced ourselves from the landscape.

" Let's go and play in the willows beside the pond," Jean suggested.

I looked up into her round rosy-cheeked face, with its halo of golden hair, and we laughed.

As fast as we could we ran for the willows. " Do you suppose we could hear her now if she called? " I asked.

Jean's answer was not as irrelevant as it sounded. " She'll likely get me to set the table, and make some muffins, and send you in to talk to him," she reflected aloud with satisfaction.

I stood up, holding a bunch of white
anemones I had just gathered in my hand
and rubbed the yellow pollen against my nose,
as I asked shyly, " Jean, what do you say when
he looks at you so hard and asks if you are
right with God? "

" I say ' yes ' every time," Jean answered,
" and then he stops worrying me, but I don't
like him to do it."

" Neither do I," I agreed.   " How does
anyone know whether they are right with
God? "

" I don't know."

" Do you suppose anybody, even Mr. Elton,
really knows? " I questioned.

Mother's voice calling, " Girls, girls," interrupted us.

Reluctantly we turned our feet houseward.
When we entered the big grey-painted kitchen,
with the flourishing red geraniums in the
window, mother, who was bustling about getting tea, stopped and said, " Aleta, go into
the parlour and talk to Mr. Elton."

" I showed him all the photos last time," I
objected.

" Then just talk to him, dear," she
answered, and her blue eyes twinkled as she
bent and kissed my forehead.

When mother asked me that way to do anything I was helpless to resist. I would have
faced a regiment of Eltons.

While Mr. Elton pumped my hand up and
down he gave me a deep, silent, searching
look, which made me squirm inwardly.

"How is Minnie?" I asked desperately,
resolved to ward off the spiritual inquisition as
long as possible. Minnie Forsyth was board-
ing with the Eltons in order to continue at a
good school, her father having been moved by
the Methodist Board to a less desirable town.
I seized upon her eagerly as a plausible subject of conversation. "Minnie is very well,
but the question is, how is Aleta?" he said
pointedly.

I understood his meaning perfectly, but pretended not to. "I'm fine," I answered, "but
I had an awfully sore throat on Monday and
one of my tonsils is swelled up yet."

He stared at me in funereal silence.

"Would you like to look at it," I offered
amiably.

He waived aside the invitation to explore
my throat. "It wasn't your body I was asking about, child; it was your immortal soul."

He had taken a seat on the horsehair sofa,
and I sat forward on the prickly edge of a

horsehair chair, one small hand on each knee, and looked at him solemnly.

He did not see, as I did, a big housefly, which, sighting his tempting bald crown from a distance, had come swooping across the room singing the Hallelujah Chorus. It circled round and round, like a hawk over a chicken, and just as he asked about my immortal soul it settled. He jumped up and rubbed it off.

" I'll run and get a piece of paper to kill it," I offered eagerly.

" Never mind, child," he called after me, but I was gone.

When I returned I chased that fly, or another, mercilessly. At first Mr. Elton looked on coldly and disapprovingly. Then he began to watch the fly and point it out to me. Finally he sprang up and snatched the swatter from my hand. Just as he flattened it against the window pane with a sharp slap mother appeared in the doorway and announced supper. My immortal soul had, for the time being, escaped the microscope.

Supper over, Mr. Elton asked for a Bible, and after reading a Psalm, he knelt down and prayed. He prayed for us all, but for me in particular, advising God that he might need to keep an especial watch over me, as I had a tendency to an undisciplined spirit. There was a desperate earnestness in his voice, and when he went on to ask the Heavenly Father to surround us all with His loving protection he brought the tears to my eyes. I peeked through my fingers at him, and his face was shining with a strange light. He had opened a pathway to his God—a narrow-minded, bigoted, dogmatic God, it is true, for his very limited intelligence was not capable of drawing a great and splendid picture of God—but his God.

The next Wednesday evening at prayer meeting he took up the lesson of the foolish virgins and pointed out that they obviously symbolized by the Presbyterians, Baptists and Church of England members. He did not bother to mention the Roman Catholics, for nobody in Souris River seriously expected them to go to heaven.

We had only one Roman Catholic family in the district, and it did seem to me hard that Mrs. Fagan should go straight down to hell when she got through raising her family, nursing her neighbours, and being jolly and kind to all us youngsters. But so they said it was

written. She did the right things, but the
poor woman did not believe the right things.
Hence her lost condition.

On the way home from meeting I said to
father, as we walked along the deep-rutted
road in the moonlight, " Did you ever hear of
such a thing as Mr. Elton calling the other
churches foolish virgins? "

Father stroked his beard with placid satisfaction as he declared, " You've got to be converted and born again before you go to
heaven, and they don't believe in it."

I looked over the shadowy rustling fields of
grain and then up to the eternal stars, and
said something which I intended to be very
personal, while appearing casual. " Some of
them are very kind to their families and
pleasant in their homes," I hinted.

Father gave a grunt of annoyance. " You
don't know what you're talking about," he
said shortly.

But I did, in a way. There must have been
a time, for I was no intellectual prodigy, when
I did not resent the assumption of infallibility
on the part of any individual or group of individuals, but I cannot remember it. Among
my earliest emotional recollections is the

resentment I felt at the self-complacency of the holiness Methodists, who visited our home, and at my father's extreme partisanship in politics.

CHAPTER VIII.

NED IS EXPELLED.

It was the second summer of the Boer War, and public feeling was inflamed with that peculiar national hysteria war breeds. I was in my fifteenth year, and Ned, eighteen and full grown, was studying for his second-class certificate. On a certain spring day, at the last recess, Ned, Pauline, Jean and I were sitting together in a group talking, when Pauline put her hand down on Ned's desk and picked up a copy of an American history, which Ned's father had brought with him from the land of his birth.

She tossed it disdainfully aside . " That book is full of lies," she declared contemptuously.

Ned flushed, but he merely reached over and took up his English history. " So is this," he said quietly.

I was dumbfounded. I had questioned my parents and the Bible, but up to that moment it had never occurred to me to doubt the English history.

Pauline grew purple. " How dare you say such a thing," she flashed at him.

" For the same reason that you dared to say the American history is full of lies; because it's true. All histories give a one-sided report of things."

I looked from one to the other of them uneasily. Ned's fair face was quiet and composed, but his grey eyes were flashing fire. Pauline beat a large, substantially shod foot excitedly on the floor. Her dark sombre face was flushed from neck to brow.

" You ought to be put in jail for saying things like that," she stammered in the excess of her agitation.

" No matter whether it is true or not," Ned said. " That's the way with you tories; you're always wanting to put somebody in jail --as if that proved anything."

" But it isn't true," Pauline declared.

Ned was provokingly cool. " How do you know? " he asked quietly.

" Because it isn't."

" That's a fine reason," he sneered.

Pauline threw up her head. " I suppose you know better than the man who wrote the history, and the Board of Education, and all the teachers," she said crushingly.

The other students who had been idling about the room now gathered around to listen to the quarrel.

" I wouldn't accept the word of any Board of Education or a million teachers," Ned said. " I'd read both sides of the question myself, and form my own conclusions. My father says that if the histories were any good they would give us translations from the leading historians in every country on international events, and leave us to judge for ourselves as to the facts."

" Your father is——"

We never heard what Ned's father was, for at that moment Mr. Magrath entered the room.

" What's all this noise about? " he demanded abruptly.

Silence fell upon us. Pauline always fought in the open. She was no tattle tale, but Minnie Forsyth spoke up. " Ned and Pauline were quarrelling because Ned said the English history was full of lies, and Pauline said it wasn't."

Magrath turned to Pauline. "Is that true? " he demanded, his squatty figure trembling with passion and his thick neck scarlet.

Pauline shoved a pencil up and down between her long fingers in silence. In her rage she had threatened Ned with jail, but when it came to the test she was unwilling, much as she disliked him, to reveal his short-coming to the super-patriot Magrath.

" Is this true, Pauline? " Magrath repeated.

" Yes, sir," Pauline answered, " but—but I don't think he meant it," she added, generously.

" Yes, I did," Ned said quietly.

Magrath turned pale. " Ned," he thundered, " take your books and go home. You're expelled."

Ned did not move.

" Did you hear me? " Magrath shouted.

" Certainly," Ned answered.

" Then why don't you obey me? "

" Because you have no authority to expel me from the school," Ned replied. It was uncanny the instinct Ned and his father had for law. They always knew to a nicety how far authority could go.

Magrath swallowed quickly. Then he turned on his heel and went to the desk. When he came back he carried an ugly black strap in his hand.

" There is something I have the authority

to do," he hissed. " I can give you a good
thrashing for dishonouring our country, you
young American upstart."

I never saw Ned so cool and dignified as he
was that afternoon. He looked Magrath
straight in the eye. " Put that thing down,"
he said in a quiet, powerful tone, " you can't
prove with that thing that the English history
is true."

Magrath wavered. I have no doubt that he
was restrained partly by Ned's supple young
muscles; partly by the fear that Tom Grant
would go to law with him, for Tom Grant
could plead a case so wittily and persuasively
before a jury that everyone avoided meeting
him in court.

At any rate he hesitated. Then he threw
back his shoulders and laughed. It was not a
very good laugh, but it served as a back paddle
in the argument.

" Very well, my smart young Socialist, I'll
leave it to the trustees to decide whether
you're to be allowed to contaminate the minds
of the other students by making seditious
speeches," And away he strutted and replaced
the strap in his desk.

Ned took his seat, the object of the cold
glances of all his associates. He turned to me.

I looked down at my book. I admired Ned, and nearly always agreed with him, but being a coward, I felt sometimes that I did not like to be associated with him in the minds of my friends.

The moment it had happened I was ashamed, and tried to catch his eye, but he did not glance my way until about four o'clock, when he gave me a cold, hard look. I felt like one of those shrivelled little peas at the end of a pod.

He stalked off by himself when school was over, and left me to walk home alone, even though he knew Barry was at home sick, and Jean was spending the night in town with May.

When I reached home mother was sewing in a low rocker by the south kitchen window, and on the white oil cloth covered table there was ranged a quantity of fragrant yellow loaves of bread.

" There's a pan of buns there, Aleta," she said, glancing up as I came back from carrying my books into the dining-room.

I helped myself to a bun and spread it with yellow butter. Then I brought a stool and sat down beside mother's knee and told her about the quarrel between Ned and Pauline.

" What do you think, mother? " I asked.

She was holding the needle between her
teeth while she took a new thread. " I don't
know," she mumbled.

Then she took the needle from her mouth,
licked the end of the thread, and holding them
at arm's length brought them together.

To my surprise she continued. " I don't
know but Ned was right. It seems to me very
likely that histories are prejudiced. They may
not say what is actually untrue, but they perhaps give a colour or implication to events
that is not warranted, in order to make our
country seem more perfect than it is."

Then I told her about having refused to look
at Ned and how mean I felt.

Mother put down her sewing and patted my
red brown head gently. " I'll tell you what
you had better do, Aleta," she said after a
little. " Put some of those buns in a bag and
take them down to Ned and his father for
supper, and tell Ned you're sorry."

I jumped up with alacrity. " And you
might take along a bottle of that maple syrup,"
she called, when I was in the pantry hunting
up a bag.

Father always grumbled that mother would
give away everything we had, and certainly

nearly half this consignment of maple syrup from Uncle Frank's farm in Ontario had gone in this way.

I went to the door. At the step I turned and looked at mother. Her round face, with its three-tier chin, was clearly outlined against the dark green foliage of the geraniums, and the sunlight, checkered by the leaves, fell across her sloping lap on to the grey-painted floor.

I went back and set my parcel on the table. Mother turned in surprise : " Did you forget something, Aleta? " she asked.

" Yes," I said, smiling, and I put my hands on either side of her face and kissed her forehead. She looked both pleased and abashed. That evening I found she had made one of my favourite dishes, a baked custard for my supper.

I remember with a singular distinctness every detail of that walk to the Grant's. It was May; that is to say it was intoxicating. There is a secret urge in Spring everywhere. Even in languid humid climes it is the season of matings and revolutions. But Spring in the north ! Air like champagne; a deluge of sunlight pouring down from cloudless blue skies; life bursting forth everywhere with an instinc-

tive knowledge of the need for speed if it is to
run its course and reproduce its kind before
the early autumn frost overtakes it. It is life
on the gallop to out-distance death. One
stands in awe before the spectacle of this
almost indecent hurry to survive.

As I followed the footpath along the barbed
wire fence, which enclosed the pasture field, I
thought with deep disgust of what had happened at school. Why couldn't I follow
straight and swiftly my own opinions as the
yellow buttercups at my feet went without self-
consciousness to their goal? Why did I find
myself apologetic when I did not agree with
the majority? When I was given a mind that
questioned everything, why was I not given a
spirit that feared nothing? Since minds came
into being that questioned things it seemed the
world needed that kind of mind. Then why
be ashamed of it? So I reasoned fruitlessly,
for the wings of my soul had been clipped in
my infancy. I had lost the power to fly while
retaining the will to rise above the clouds of
bigotry and prejudice.

*   *   *   *   *

The yard about the Grant's cottage was alive
with high-stepping speckled Plymouth Rock
hens, scratching backward, now and again,

and pecking about daintily. One was even reconnoitring the kitchen through the partly open door.

The bright sunshine in the room increased the dreariness of its aspect. The greasy stove had a pot of porridge on the back. Pans were set out on chairs around the room, and the table was full of dirty dishes.

I rolled up my sleeves and set to work to make a fire. Then I began to wash up the dishes, expecting every moment that Ned would come in, but I had finished them, and swept and mopped the floor, and still there was no sign of Ned.

I was determined to see him and make it up, so I began to get supper. I had just finished setting the table when I heard his step at the door.

He stopped short when he saw me. " Hello, Aleta," he exclaimed in surprise.

It was my turn to be amazed. " Then you're not angry with me? " I asked shyly.

Ned twisted his cap in his hands. " I was at first," he admitted, " but afterward when I thought it over I saw that you had not been thinking about that matter of the histories the way I had. You couldn't be expected to see it at once."

I was silent while a struggle went on inside.
At last I spoke. " I hate to tell you, Ned," I
said, " but it wasn't because I minded about
the history that I didn't look at you." I
picked up a knife and made trails on the red
damask cloth with it. " Just for a minute I—
I—was ashamed," I confessed with chagrin.

Ned was silent.

Without raising my eyes I went on. " You
won't understand. You're fearless. You
don't mind what people think of you. But I
do; I don't like being against people."

Still Ned was silent.

I looked up and saw him smiling. " I
know," he said, " I've sometimes been
ashamed of dad, and of his being a Socialist."

" And your dad such a dear old man," I
exclaimed, in a shocked voice.

Then we both laughed.

" We're in the same boat, Aleta," Ned
said, " we'll always be against the popular
side, so we may as well make up our minds to
stand by each other."

He came close up to me, slipped his arm
about my shoulders and looked down into my
eyes with a queer expression.

I was startled. I looked Ned over with a

new vision, from his boots to his smoothly
parted silkily dark hair. His upper lip was
blue. He had begun to shave. Ned was a
man.

I looked down and giggled. It had flashed
upon me all at once that I was a woman.

Ned closed his short-fingered, work-
roughened hand over mine.

A great scraping was heard at the door. It
was Ned's father come home from work. We
blushed and sprang apart.

That night when I was going to bed I spent
a long time sitting before my mirror. The
person reflected there was not very satis-
factory : short, stubby, a round sallow face
with irregular features, and tanned. But
there was my hair, long silky curls of red
brown clustering about my head, and my dark
brown eyes, which some people told me were
beautiful. I brushed my hair until it crackled
and stood out about my head in a shining
cloud.

The next morning, as I was helping mother
get the breakfast, I said : " Do you know anything that will take off tan? "

Mother looked at me long and hard, almost
resentfully, I thought.

" Buttermilk," she answered, shortly.

* * * * *

They expelled Ned from school, thereby
proving the accuracy of the English history,
and his father planned to send him, for the
balance of the term, to Winnipeg, where he
meant to enter law school in the autumn anyway.

Ned came the evening before he left to say
good-bye to us. He stayed only a little while.
Father and Jean had never been particularly
friendly to him, but even mother was a little
cool, which I thought queer, since she had
said she thought Ned was probably right.

But Barry brought him his greatest treasure,
a knife with a corkscrew, several broken
blades, and a good one. He put it diffidently
into Ned's hand.

" What's this? " Ned asked quickly.

Barry blushed and rubbed his close-cropped
head up and down against Ned's arm. " It's
for you," he answered proudly.

" Why, thanks old man, that's awfully good
of you, but I think you'll be needing it more
than I will and you'd better keep it."

Barry took it quietly and slipped it into the
back pocket of his funny little overalls.

I frowned. I knew that Ned's motive was

kindly, for he knew how much Barry prized the knife, but the refusal of the gift seemed indelicate.

When Ned had said his farewells and I walked out with him to the gate, he said, "Wasn't it nice of the kid to offer me his knife? But of course I couldn't take it, he's so stuck on it himself."

"I think you made a mistake, Ned," I objected.

"Do you think so, Aleta?" he asked quickly. "I'm sorry if I've annoyed you. I seem to have got in wrong all round. I suppose there are lots of things a fellow doesn't get on to when he grows up without a mother or sisters."

Ned was a very little boy at that moment and very sorry for himself, but there was something infinitely appealing about him. I glimpsed faintly what it meant for a boy to start out in the world without any woman to pet him and fuss over him.

So I held out both my hands. "Haven't I been almost as good as a sister to you, Ned?"

He took my hands in his and looked at me with the expression his face had worn the week before.

" Better," he said, decidedly. " I'm
awfully glad you're not my sister."

" Why? " I asked, provocatively.

" Will you kiss me, Aleta? " he demanded,
suddenly.

I drew my hands away and shook my head.
I wanted to kiss him, too, but something held
me back. The puritanical may be inclined to
put it down to maidenly modesty, but I think
myself it was prudishness.

*   *   *   *   *

When I was sitting brushing my hair that
night, Barry came in in his nighty. I saw
that he carried in his hand his rejected gift.

" I guess it's not much good of a knife," he
suggested, anxiously, disillusion dimming the
smiling brightness of his dear blue eyes.

I held open my arms. " Come here,
sonny," I said.

When he had come and cuddled against me,
I said : " Did you think Ned didn't like your
knife, Barry? "

Barry turned his back to me and dug his
little pink toes into the rag carpet.
" Uh-huh."

" You were wrong then, for Ned told me
outside that he didn't take it because he knew
you liked it so much."

" Then you think it's a good knife."

" Of course."

" Would you like to have it? "

" Would I like the pot of gold at the end of
the rainbow? "

Barry clapped his hands jubilantly. " Then
I'll give it to you."

After a thoughtful pause he suggested, " I
suppose you wouldn't mind lending it to me
now and again? "

" Not a bit," I agreed readily. " I'll leave
it on this table and we can both use it."

So I did, and often it disappeared, but was
always returned in the evening. Sometimes,
to this day, when I put my hand down to the
bottom of a certain old workbox it touches
that knife, and my heart goes still, and a black
cloud settles down upon my spirit.

CHAPTER IX.

The Storm Wind Again.

It was a winter night; not unlike the one
on which Barry came into the world. Our
house trembled and creaked as the north wind,
charged with snow, came roaring down the
road allowance and broke, with an impotent
shriek, against the rattling windows.

But this time there was no long wait for the
doctor. He had been in the house since morning. Barry lay very still on the bed, except
for the heavy breathing of pneumonia.
Mostly he lay in a stupor, but whenever he
grew brighter he asked for mother and me, so
we stayed near at hand.

The still excitement of a serious sickness
makes a queer halting place in one's
experience. All the usual things give place to
the unusual. That day we spoke with hushed
voices, and walked softly even in the kitchen,
where we could not possibly have disturbed
Barry.

Mother was dark about the eyes and quiet;
father was silent, and Jean pale. As for me,
something had happened that morning that

had completely upset me. Perhaps that day would have been less awful if I had shared it with the others. I tried several times, but my lips refused to do my bidding.

I had been left alone with Barry for a few minutes when he roused up and asked for some water. I put my arm around him and raised him up, for he was very weak. As I laid him back on the pillow he whispered something.

" What is it, Barry? " I asked.

He repeated it, and this time I caught the words, " Does it hurt much to die? "

" No," I answered, my voice trembling, " but you're not going to die." Then I was seized with panic, and repeated wildly, " You're not going to die; you're not going to die. You wouldn't leave Aleta, would you, Barry? "

He was sinking again into a stupor, but I think he answered " No."

Mother came in just then with a bottle of medicine in her hand. " Mother," I said, drawing in a long sobbing breath. She laid a plump hand on my arm. " What is it, dear? " she asked anxiously.

I shook my head, went to the window, and stood looking through a clear spot at the top

of a thickly frosted pane upon the flat white
desolation, which spread out unbroken to
meet the distant cold sky.

What had made the child think of death, I
questioned, and could find no answer. Nobody would have spoken to him about it.
Was it intuition? Was it premonition? I
did not weep, but the landscape seemed completely blotted out. I saw before me, instead
of the brilliant winter world, a long, dark
avenue, where neither the sun nor the moon
nor the stars did shine, and where there was
only a dim grey gate at the end leading into
the garden of death. That was life as it looked
without Barry.

The doctor came at eleven. He took
Barry's temperature, felt his pulse, and shook
his head.

" I believe the crisis will come some time
to-day or this evening," he replied, when
questioned, and announced his intention of
staying.

I had not noticed until that day that Jean
was a woman. It came to me when I saw the
doctor, who was young and single, give her an
admiring glance, which passed her by un-
noticed. She was quite unconscious of his

approval, as her thoughts were all with the little brother battling for his life upstairs.

She was a great comfort to everyone at that time. A born housekeeper, she took things into her own hands; tidied the house, as usual, prepared tempting hot meals, and coaxed us one after another to eat them. It is a blessed thing in the house of sickness to have someone about who translates sorrow into service.

As for me, I hardly know how I spent that day. It seems to me I moved about in a dark shadow made deeper by the storm that overspread the sky in the late afternoon, and that before me there moved always that pathetic little question, " Does it hurt much to die? "

When night settled in, and the storm, grown to a blizzard, roared and shrieked about the house, a superstitious fear took possession of me. Barry had come into the world in a blizzard.   Had the storm wind come back for him?

The hours crept away, and as the evening wore on, Dr. Graham stayed continuously at Barry's side, looking anxious and feeling his pulse very frequently.

About ten o'clock he laid the little hand

back on the bed and looked at us strangely.

     *   *   *   *   *

The sun streaming in through the thickly-frosted window and turning it into a sheet of glittering diamonds, looked cheerful. I sat up in bed briskly. I had had an awful dream. It had been that Barry was gone. A terrible dream.

I caught my breath suddenly. Did I remember, or was it a nightmare, the little hand being laid back on the bed, and that I walked the floor for the rest of the night, and all the next day tearless and silent, until they had sent for the doctor, who had given me a glass of milk with a queer taste.

I remembered.

After that for a long time I beat the wings of my will, which would not have it so, against the absolute fact that it was so. What seemed hours later I put on my clothes and crept downstairs. As I was passing the parlour door I saw something white standing by the window. I stopped short; went on again; turned back and drew near to that small white box. Barry's face, waxy and still, smiled up at me. His question was answered. It does not hurt to die—only to live.

I knelt down beside that little white coffin, laid my head on it and wept. Presently I felt two arms slipped about me, and my head was gently moved from the hard coffin to a friendly shoulder. I looked up into Pauline's kind, brown eyes. She did not tell me, as Minnie Forsyth had tried to do the day before, that Barry was better dead—poor comfort that when the heart was crying out for him. We wept quietly together, and the memory of that morning beside Barry's coffin keeps Pauline from quite hating me now, and me from hating her. We would not have believed then that the day would ever come when we would look the other way when we met on the street.

Everybody went out to the graveyard, and when we came back the chairs were all in rows, as they had been for the service; the fire was out, and some of the men who had come to the funeral had missed the ashpan of the kitchen stove and spat on the floor around it. In this dreary house, and on that cold winter day, I started life all over again at sixteen without Barry.

CHAPTER X.

AGNOSTICISM.

When Ned came home from Winnipeg the next June we made a great discovery. It was on a Sunday evening after church. All we girls walked out of the service with downcast eyes, in spite of which we managed to see the youths who detached themselves from their fellows, and proudly yet nervously approached us with uplifted hats.

Ned joined us, and after the custom of the village we turned to stroll down the most densely maple shaded street, for the long northern summer evening has only well begun at eight o'clock.

When we had adjusted our pace to that of the couples fore and aft so as to be out of ear-shot of both, Ned turned to me and asked, "What do you think of Christianity, Aleta?"

"I think it is perhaps the purest system of morals the world has yet evolved," I answered patly, greatly to his surprise and my own, for I was hardly conscious that I had been thinking about Christianity at all.

Then we held what the Indians would call a pow-wow over our unbelief. We went step by step along that path that had led us to our present conclusions, and to our great delight found them to be identical. In half an hour we had disposed of the inspiration of the Bible, the Divinity of Christ, and put a big blue question mark over the immortality of the soul. We felt that we had done a good night's work and went home in a highly elated mood.

I said good-night to Ned and went in past Jean and Dr. Graham, who were standing at the gate talking. An hour or two later I glanced out of the window and saw them kissing in the moonlight. I was disgusted.

When Jean mentioned Dr. Graham the next day I said : " I think he is horribly soft and very homely."

Jean flushed angrily. " He's much better looking than Ned, at any rate," she declared.

" Well, I don't think I ever said Ned was good looking, did I? " was my reply, and Jean was baffled.

After that I was mean enough never to miss a chance of saying something unpleasant about Dr. Graham, for I was furious at the idea that

Jean might get married and I would be shut
out from her life.

        *   *   *   *   *

The next Sunday night I declined to go to
church. " Why not? " mother asked.

I was on the point of telling her how foolish
it all was, but something held me back. I
could blast anybody's faith but mother's. In-
sufferable little egoist that I was to suppose
that the walls of my mother's faith, which had
stood through all the storms of life, would fall
at one puny blast from my trumpet. But I
really thought I was sparing her a great dis-
illusionment by answering merely that I was
tired.

Ned came over later and we sat on the
verandah steps and wordily patronised people
who attended churches.

Ned was sitting in the sunlight, and I where
the shadows of the house fell over my white
muslin dress and black Oxford shoes. In one
of the pauses of the conversation I studied
him thoughtfully. His strong, medium-sized
figure had filled out wonderfully during the
past year, and since he had been to Winnipeg
he was always clean and neatly dressed.

My concentrated gaze made him turn his

rugged face towards me, and he smiled,
revealing a row of large white teeth.

" It's wonderful how well we suit each
other, isn't it, Aleta? " he asked, sidling over
nearer me on the steps.

I sidled a little away, I couldn't just say why.
But he kept coming closer. He took my hand
and pressed it and looked at me with far other
thoughts than of religion shining in his eyes.
I squirmed and drew my hand away, for the
woman in me was still sound asleep, and that
look of the man seeking his mate, which I
saw in Ned's eyes, made me uncomfortable.

" Don't you like me, Aleta? " he questioned.

" Why, yes," I answered, " but we're too
young for that. I want to do ever so many
things before——" I broke off abruptly and
studied the clear horizon flushed by the sun-
set.

" What's the use of starting a lot of things
and having to give them up when you get
married? " Ned objected.

" Maybe I wouldn't give them up," I said.

" You'd have to," he returned flatly.

I frowned. I was very immature, and had
thought very little about the marriage rela-
tionship, but this speech of Ned's grated un-
pleasantly upon me.

CHAPTER XI.
McNair.

It was twelve years later that I was riding home to Winnipeg, one winter afternoon, on a train that crept slowly over the creaking frosty rails. From my chair in the parlor car I watched the smooth fields of snow slip past the train windows, the while I enlarged upon the points I had not made in an address I had delivered upon woman suffrage in an outlying village the evening before.

While I was adding wit and grace retrospectively to a speech which had been dull enough in reality, the train slowed down with a harsh grinding sound, jerked us nearly out of our seats, and stopped.

A huge man unfolded himself from the seat next mine, rose up to a prodigious height and breadth; shook his brown tweed trousers down over his tan boots; walked with a slow, echoless tread to the door, and went out.

When he returned he was carrying in his hand one of the city papers. He spread it out on his knee and we began to read it. I had covered the headings of the big murder trial, and was into the latest political scandal when he turned over.

He insists to this day that I gave a sharp exclamation of annoyance, which is, of course, absurd. I did nothing of the kind, but however that may be he looked up, our eyes met, and we smiled.

" Did I turn too soon? "he asked mildly, but with a twinkle in his eye.

" Just three more lines," I said laughing, and he turned back and let me see them. So we shared the paper between us, and from that we went on to talk of books, plays and the like, and he dug about in his capacious pockets and brought out several little scrap books with poems and snatches of philosophy. While I read them he watched me with eager grey eyes, which in their boyishness belied his otherwise mature appearance. He seemed oddly anxious that I should not think them foolish.

On one of these excursions into an inside pocket he brought out a photograph with the book he was after, hesitated a moment, then handed it to me with a smile. " That's my boy Colin," he said pridefully, and watched my face harder than ever for approval.

My heart sank. It was a shock to me to find that the stranger was married.

"He's a nice boy," I said coldly, "but he doesn't look much like you."

As if in answer to my thoughts the stranger explained quickly, "I am only his guardian, but I could not think more of him if he were my own son."

"He's a manly looking little chap," I amended cordially, and I smiled at the photograph of a grave little lad of about thirteen years.

The stranger went on to explain about him. "His mother died when he was born, and his father when he was three, and when his father, who was my dearest friend, was dying he sent for me and said, 'McNair, I'm going to leave Colin to you, to raise like your own son.'

"That was back in Scotland," he concluded. "I suppose you guessed I was a Scotchman."

I smiled. "Guessed?" And the man had been filling the car with burrs ever since he had begun to speak.

But what had I heard about some McNair lately? Memory came in a flash. "Would you be the Mr. McNair who has come up from the East to edit the Rural Review?" I asked.

" The same," he admitted, surprised.

" Then you and I are sworn enemies. I'm on the Country Register."

Memory came to his aid also. " You wouldn't be Miss Aleta Dey? " he suggested, hesitatingly, as one unwilling to accuse anybody unjustly.

I nodded assent, and I never saw a more disappointed looking man. " Then you're a suffragette."

" Gist," I corrected, gently but firmly.

He paid no attention to the distinction, which was swallowed up in the general disaster, but sat silently glowering into the dusk, his face drawn down into deep haggard lines as he chewed away at the amber stem of his unlighted pipe.

At last he turned to me, and his face brightened with a most engaging smile. " Anyway, you've good notions about books," he said, dwelling charitably upon my one redeeming quality. " Let's go and have a bite to eat, and by that time we'll be in the city," and he stuffed the pipe in his pocket and led the way to the dining car.

When we parted at the station he put out his big hand and I laid my wee one in it, and I cannot tell you how it happened, but a thrill,

such as I had never experienced in my life
before, passed up my right arm and down my
left side, and I knew, without looking at the
great man, who was standing there holding
my hand as if it was a parcel I had given him
for keeps, that he felt the thrill, too.

" I'd be glad to have the pleasure of your
acquaintance, if I may," he was saying in his
quaint old-fashioned manner.

I took my hand away at last, being driven
to it by a sense of decency, and searched in
my handbag for a card, which I gave him.

" You may call on me some evening at that
address, if you care to," I said. And so we
parted.

Had my father been alive he would have
been scandalised to see me go home and hurry
straight to the rouge pot, which was requisi-
tioned only on such state occasions as came
when I was all tired out and looking my
worst. I applied it unsparingly, and then
dabbed myself with powder until even mother
would have been shocked if she had been
present, which luckily she was not, having
gone, after father's death, to help nurse the
babies of Jean and Dr. Graham, who were
married and settled in Souris River, next door
to May Ransome and her husband.

I looked at myself critically in the glass. It was a great improvement on Nature's handi-work, but it wouldn't do. The improvement was too obvious. So I went out to Mrs. Fleming's sink and scrubbed my face clean of the mess. When I came back to my parlour bedroom I looked my wardrobe over carefully and found I had not a decent dress to put on. I decided to get myself a new one the very next day, which I did.

CHAPTER XII.

A Tilt About Socialism.

When I was considering the new dress, Pauline hailed me from the aisle and hastened to join me. She was a tall young woman now, and head of the children's department of the public library.

" Isn't this luck? " she exclaimed. " Something's burst in the steam plant, so we are closed up, and I was looking for somebody to play with. Let's go . . and . . . have . . . . some . . . . . tea."

The last sentence died out, as I have tried to indicate, when her glance fell upon the dresses the clerk had ranged before me.

" Why, Aleta," she exclaimed, " you're not buying a summer dress at this season of the year, are you? "

I did not want to explain to Pauline that there are occasions, even during the cold weather, when such a dress is useful, especially if light colours are more becoming to one than dark; for example, when one is receiving a caller informally in the evening.

But I merely said, " It's the last day of February, Pauline."

" Yes; but, my dear, you'll not get any wear out of a dress like that before June, and then they will be less expensive. Come and look at these silks."

I had great respect for Pauline's opinion about clothes, for she is twice as clever as I in the matter of dress, so I followed her. She tried to foist a sober blue and black thing upon me, but I would have none of it, and stood out for a warm Burgundy, which Pauline thought too dear, but as I was paying for it I had my way. And the next day I went back and bought the pink muslin, too, though I would not like Pauline to find that out. She thinks I do not save enough.

When we had completed the purchase of the taffeta dress, Pauline and I hunted up one of those pretty little tea rooms, which make Winnipeg a decent place in which to live.

" Well, how did you get along at your meeting? " she asked, as she finished writing the order on the tiny pad.

" I made a great speech on the train coming home," I admitted, with a laugh.

Pauline laughed, too, as she threw aside her furs. She was an ardent suffragist. In our outlook upon public life that was the one point of contact between us.

" There were a couple of Socialists there who got up and fired questions at me about the capitalist system, which I was not in a position to answer," I said.

" They make me sick," Pauline declared, " with their everlasting ' Capitalist System ' and ' Class conscious workers.' A lot of ignorant beggars, too lazy to get out and earn a decent living for themselves, so they want to grab what honest people make."

" There's more to Socialism than that, Pauline," I objected. " Some of those people are poor because they have been so weakened by malnutrition in their youth, and so hampered by the lack of an education that they haven't a chance in the struggle for existence."

" I don't believe it," Pauline said, flatly.

I looked at her with a feeling of hopelessness.

" Have you no imagination," I asked, indignantly, " that you seem incapable of sympathising with any injustice except this matter of woman suffrage, which touches you personally. Do you intend to go through life saying, ' I don't believe it ' about everything it would make you uncomfortable to face? "

Pauline's face took on that patronising, supercilious expression, which always made

Ned want to strangle her, and she said,
" Don't give me one of Ned's lectures second-
hand, Aleta. It's bad enough to have to
endure the first edition when one can't escape
it."

Perhaps it was Pauline's commanding
physical presence which enabled her to seem
to put me completely in the wrong, when the
only answer she could make to any facts I
offered for her consideration was, " I don't
believe it."

She was the most perfect type I have ever
known of established authority, frequently
benevolent, always unimaginative, and so sure
of herself that if such a thing as a dispute
between herself and God were possible she
would know that God was mistaken.

I, on the other hand, had often the unpleasant aggressiveness of timidity; the self-
assertion which frequently arises from being
driven by an unknown urge to defy authority
of which one stands in awe.

I have always felt that I owe that fear of
authority to my stern upbringing, to my
father's cruel chastisements in particular, and
I have never conquered my resentment of it.
So when my father died I shed no tears. It
would have been black hypocrisy to weep for

the man who whipped my spirit into servility.

I suppose there is no unpardonable sin, but if there were I am sure it would be this, for authority so to enchain a man's soul with fear that he loses the power " to draw the Thing as he sees it, for the God of the Things as they are."

CHAPTER XIII.

A Visitor.

It was a week later that I was called to the telephone, and a deep, rich voice said over the wire, " This is McNair speaking."

I beamed upon that telephone and said, " Oh, yes, Mr. McNair."

" I was thinking that if you were going to be disengaged this evening I would call upon you," he continued.

I cancelled in intention a walk I had planned to take, and assured him I was quite free and would be delighted to see him.

As I went home in the sharp frosty darkness I gathered up tasty things for refreshments on the way, and arrived there I hunted out a pair of white silk stockings, and swept and dusted the room till it shone, and laid a fire in the grate, and bathed and put on my finest and daintiest things.

After dinner, of which Mrs. Fleming complained that I ate hardly a mouthful, I slipped into my own room and donned the white silk stockings and my white kid pumps, and lastly the delicate rose muslin frock which set off my

dark hair and complexion to the best possible
advantage.

At last I sat down to wait and looked about
the room with a feeling of genuine satisfaction. Little by little I had eliminated Mrs.
Fleming from the place. At the last house
cleaning I had persuaded her to let me have a
warm buff kalsomine on the walls instead of
the brightly medallioned paper she had in
mind, and a plain brown grass rug in exchange
for the bright green leaves and pink flowers of
the tapestry, which fitted the measure of her
purse. And one by one I had carried up to
the back bedroom the ugly plush-covered
chairs and substituted for them cretonned-
cushioned rockers and easy chairs of willow.

So that to-night as I looked about the room,
fragrant with pots of crocus, and blue, pink
and heliotrope hyacinths, which filled the
sills of the windows at the side of the room,
and overflowed on to the top of the bookcase
and table, I had a feeling of genuine pride in
this little place, which was all I had of home
in the world.

I rose and moved the tea table up beside the
fire, and took the copper tray, filled with dull
green dishes, from the top of the bookcase and
set it on the table. Then I stood back to

admire the effect. At that moment the bell
rang. I touched a match to the firewood in
the grate and hurried to the door.

There was McNair, bigger than I had
remembered him. Again my little palm was
laid against his huge one, and again a thrill
went through me as he closed his fingers over
mine.

He stooped his head to enter the doorway
of my room, and looked about him in pleased
surprise. "You're very cosy here, aren't
you?" he remarked, and I cannot say how
gratified I was that he thought my place
pretty.

I watched him, smiling to myself, as he let
himself down circumspectly into the biggest
and strongest of my chairs, which at that was
a poor fit for him.

As it groaned under his weight he gave me
an apprehensive look, and inquired anxiously,
"Do you think it will hold?"

I expressed my confidence in the furniture
and he leaned back in the chair; stretched his
long legs out to the fire; put his hand instinctively into the pocket of his coat, and brought
it quickly away empty, remembering his man-
ners in the nick of time.

" Wouldn't you like to smoke? " I asked, rightly interpreting the action.

He beamed on me, drew out his pipe and filled it, dribbling the tobacco carelessly on the rug, as a man is apt to do when he has been a bachelor too long, and had women paid to run around after him and keep silent about the trouble he makes.

He puffed hard at his pipe for a few seconds; took it from his mouth; watched the smoke curl slowly ceilingward. Then he turned to me with that winning smile of his, " You're sure you don't mind? " he asked.

" Not in the least," I lied cheerfully. As a matter of fact tobacco smoke does not agree with me very well, giving me a headache if taken in too large quantities, but I wouldn't have had him know that for any consideration. I wanted him to like me, and I knew that if it were a choice between that pipe and me I wouldn't have a chance in the world. The lies we women tell at such times! But God knows we have to or we would never get ourselves mates, so He overlooks it.

And now, being thoroughly comfortable, McNair turned to me, and I knew that he was aware that I was looking very well in my rose gown, and very likely he was thinking what a

sensible little woman I was to buy such simple
dainty things. I could have told him, if I'd
had a mind to, that the more simple a
woman's clothes look the harder her husband
is going to have to work to pay for them, but
as The Preacher says, " He that increaseth
knowledge increaseth sorrow."

I had planned before he came that I would
talk to McNair about sensible things like
politics (at that time I believed politics to be
a rational subject) and let him see how intelligent I was, so I was amazed to hear myself
saying, " How do you like my new dress? "

It was all wrong. I did not want McNair to
know it was a new dress, in the first place
lest he should think I had bought it on his
account, which I had, and in the second
because it was frivolous. But from the
moment we met in the train McNair and I
fitted together so comfortably that all the pro-
prieties of a new acquaintanceship fell away
from us naturally.

He looked surprised and oddly pleased at
the question.

" I was just thinking what a pretty gown it
is," he answered gravely, " though I don't
know much about women's things. I was left
an orphan when I was a little shaver and went

to work young. About all the education I ever got was at night school, and through reading books I picked up by myself."

With this glimpse of his past I began to understand the secret of McNair's charm as well as his shy diffidence about the queer medley of things he liked, and his boyish eagerness to share them with someone.

" And since I've grown up," McNair began again, paused, drew his mouth down gloomily at the corners, and stared silently into the fire. It struck me that he had one of the saddest faces I had ever seen.

At last he raised his head and looked at me with a deep melancholy in his gentle grey eyes. " I may be obliged to explain to you some day why I have had so little to do with women since I have grown up," he said. " Perhaps I ought to do so now, but I don't see that it would do any good."

" Mr. McNair," I returned, in answer to the implied question of his tone, " there is nothing about you which I am not willing to take on trust."

He looked exceedingly pleased and grateful. " That is very good of you," he said, in a deep rich voice.

I could not see that it was, since it seemed

to me that the whole atmosphere of the man breathed a clean, wholesome outlook upon life. That is still my opinion, though I now know the two things that he had in mind when he asked the question.

He now reached down into his pocket and brought out one of the old classics and read me a passage from it, and that started an argument, and then McNair, being Scotch, was in his element. We chased each other up hill and down dale with words, and whenever I pursued him too hotly he would put his fingers together thoughtfully, look at me with a smile and say, " I wonder."

In which circumstances there was nothing to be done but smile back, and maybe give him another cup of tea or a sandwich, which last he would wave in my face by way of emphasizing a point.

CHAPTER XIV.

NED AGAIN.

On a certain unlucky night Ned met McNair at my room. Several times they had missed each other by an hour or two, but at last they came together. And they clashed immediately. An election was imminent and Ned was working night and day for an independent candidate, while McNair was throwing all his influence on the side of the Conservatives. After I had introduced them there was a pause for a moment before Ned turned to me with the question :

" Did you see that article about Fraser in this morning's ' Times '? "

As it happened I had not seen it.

McNair chuckled. " I think that was the wittiest bit of writing I have seen in a long time," he declared. " I wonder who did it? "

I looked anxiously at Ned's dark frowning face as he glared with dilating nostrils at McNair.

When he spoke his voice trembled with suppressed temper. " You thought it witty, did you? I thought it the most contemptible

example of mud-slinging we've had in the
campaign, and I can't say any worse of it than
that."

So they began a sharply contested battle on
the political situation, Ned appealing to me
several times for support, which I gave un-
equivocally. It seemed to me that no one but
an intense partisan would support the side
McNair was advocating, and I did not hesitate
to say so. It is true I loved McNair and I
wanted him to love me, but I could not pre-
tend to be other than I was to gain that end.

I noticed that the first time Ned called me
Aleta, McNair looked quickly from him to
me, and from that time forward he was more
sarcastic in his arguments than I had ever
known him to be. Altogether it was a most
unpleasant hour before McNair, who had an
engagement at the office, rose to leave.

I went to the outside door with him, and
when I gave him my hand to say good-night
he pressed it very gently, releasing it with a
caressing touch of each finger, which brought
a flood of colour to my face.

When I returned to the room Ned exclaimed in a tone of deep disgust, " Did you
ever see such a hopeless reactionary? How
do you stand him? "

"We need some brakes on the wheel of progress, Ned," I apologised for McNair.

He yawned contemptuously behind his hand. "It's not much of a job, though, for a full-sized man. He might leave that to women."

"Why, Ned," I exclaimed indignantly, "I thought you were a feminist." Ned was a leading light in our suffrage organisation.

He had the grace to blush. "So I am," he protested quickly; "don't be cross, Aleta."

"But I am cross," I answered. "Theoretically you believe in the equality of the sexes, but practically you do not feel that we are equal any more than McNair does. If you had a wife you would bully her with the worst of them."

Ned was sitting stooped over, with his knees spread out and his hands clasped between them. At that he turned and gave me a straight look with his piercing grey eyes. "I wish you would give me a chance to prove that you are wrong in that, Aleta," he said quietly, but with a deep seriousness.

"Please don't—Ned," I stammered, twisting my handkerchief in my hands. "I—I don't want to hurt you again."

"All right," he replied, with a quick intake of his breath, " I'll just wait until you do learn to care for me."

He must have read something in my face, for he stopped short.

" Unless," he suggested, " unless you have learned to care for someone else? "

The colour mounted to my forehead, as I nervously smoothed the handkerchief on my lap.

" Is it McNair? "

The words fell upon the silence with such a queer hoarse sound that I turned anxiously to look at Ned. His face was blanched, and there was a drawn look about his lips.

Another wave of colour surged over my face as I nodded my head slowly.

After a long silence Ned cleared his throat and asked, " Do you know anything about this man's life, Aleta? "

" Very little," I answered, " and I am not willing to know any more than he is prepared to tell me himself."

I think that speech, more than anything I could have said, convinced Ned of my infatuation for McNair. He went away shortly, and from that time forward came to see me less often.

That night as I lay in bed I was filled with

wonder at the criss-crosses of life. I agreed with Ned's opinions on most things, nearly everything, in fact, and I knew him to be one of the most upright men God ever made. A seer of visions, he went more than half way to meet progress, so that as a citizen he far outshone McNair, but—but—well, I had never found myself measuring how far my head would come up supposing I stood within the circle of his arms, or trembling at the imagined pressure of his lips on mine. I have never stood in McNair's arms either, but if I had I know that my head would hardly have come to the level of his heart.

CHAPTER XV.
COLIN REFUSES TO COME.

It happened that Mrs. Fleming, who was a widow and childless, had an invalid cousin, with whom she took tea every Sunday evening, and that left me alone to get tea for myself, so I arranged to have McNair come for this meal, and I asked him to bring the boy Colin along.

The first Sunday night he said the boy had a toothache, and the next a headache, and the third a toe so sore he could not get his boot on, and I knew by the way McNair told me of these disablements that he took them all in good faith.

" Why, McNair," I said the third night, " he doesn't want to come."

McNair opened his eyes very wide and drew his face down solemnly, " Do you think not? " he asked. " Why do you say that? "

" Because they are all my old Sunday school excuses," I laughed.

McNair frowned; put his table napkin on the cloth, squeezing it all in a bunch under his big hand, and rose from the table.

"Where are you going?" I asked, as he marched with that slow stately step of his out into the hall.

He did not answer, so I got up and ran after him and caught him just as he was going out of the door with his hat jammed down on his head.

"Where are you going?" I asked again, catching him by the coat and holding him.

"I'm going to fetch the young rascal. He'll not insult your hospitality like that."

"If you do I'll lock you both out when you come back," I threatened.

"Why?"

"Come indoors, so that the neighbours won't see me trying to keep you here against your will, and I'll tell you."

When we were seated I rested my chin in the palm of my hand and looked across the table at McNair, who with his stiff, lightish hair all awry was stirring his cup of tea violently.

"Don't you know you couldn't have brought Colin?" I asked. "No, you couldn't," I insisted, as he opened his mouth to protest. "You might have used your great physical force, or your power as his guardian to bring Colin's body, but his goodwill would

have escaped you. That would likely have
been turned to hatred towards me for having
been, indirectly, the cause of this outrage
against his personal liberty."

I told him of the cruel punishments to
which I had been subjected as a child, and
how I had learned from them that real power
over the mind of anyone is in inverse ratio
to the use of physical force. He listened sympathetically, for McNair is that rare member
of the human species, a person who listens
with enthusiasm.

" And so I don't want you to bring Colin
by force," I concluded, " for I want your boy
to love me."

As I said it I blushed and looked down and
took up a spoon from beside my plate and
began to make lines on the cloth with it.

McNair was silent so long that I looked up,
and was surprised to see him sitting in a tense
attitude, sideways to the table, his right hand
closed upon a crumpled napkin, his left
clenched on his knee, and his face drawn
down into deep haggard lines, while he stared
out of the window with that sad expression I
had often surprised in his eyes.

He must have felt my eyes upon him, for he
turned to me with a wistful smile and said

gently, " I was taking for granted that he
wouldn't be able to help it when he came to
know you."

Then indeed I blushed furiously, and waited
breathlessly for him to say more. But he only
took his pipe from his pocket, lit it and puffed
gloomily into the twilight. However, as I
went about the task of clearing up I felt that
his eyes often followed me.

Before he went home that evening we had
made a plan for capturing Colin. The next
Sunday evening he was not to come to tea,
but I would meet them on the street going to
the restaurant for dinner, and be asked to
join them.

They were to be coming up the north side
of Portage Avenue, between Garry and Har-
grave Streets at ten minutes to six.

" Mind you're not late," was McNair's
parting injunction.

CHAPTER XVI.

WOOING COLIN.

Sunday came, a bright April day, but raw. I watched the time carefully so that I should not have to wait long on the street and yet should not miss them.

And I walked slowly and then fast, and the jeweller's clock said ten to six and then five to six, and still there was no sign of McNair and the boy. I had worn my spring coat, because it was more becoming than my fur one, and I was nearly perishing.

Suddenly I was hailed from across the street, and there was McNair beckoning to me. And he was alone.

"Woman," he exclaimed indignantly, when I had come within speaking distance, "don't you know the difference between the north and the south side of a street?"

McNair was blue with cold, too, and very angry with me, but I had no time to think of that yet. "Where's Colin?" I asked, deeply disappointed that he was not there.

"I sent him back for a pocket handkerchief I did not want," McNair said, "and if you'll

go around that corner and down one block
and back, I think we'll meet according to
plan."

So it turned out all right in spite of my mistake and I met Colin.

When McNair said, " This is my boy Colin,
of whom I've been speaking to you," I put
out my hand and he touched his cap, and
allowed me to hold a limp, cold, unresponsive
fist for a fraction of a minute before he drew
it away and thrust it into the pocket of his
bloomer trousers.

As McNair asked me in his best imitation
of an off-hand manner to have tea with them,
I noticed a disappointed expression pass over
the boy's face as if he had been counting on
having McNair to himself this evening. Yet
I was selfish enough to go.

At first I talked mostly to McNair, but afterwards I turned to the boy, a lad tall for his
thirteen years, and with a dour Scotch face. I
tried to discover what he liked, and experi-
mented with boating, baseball and tennis, but
he would merely answer ' yes ' and ' no ' to
my questions and look down again at his plate.

At last I gave him up in despair, and, turning again to McNair, I began to speak of an
historical pageant that was to be given the

next week at the exhibition grounds, and of
the aviator who was going to take part in it.

Colin put down his knife and leaned forward.

"Are you interested in aviation, Colin?"
I asked, turning to him quickly.

"A—a—little," he stammered, taken un-
awares.

"So am I," I said heartily. Then a great
inspiration came to me.

"Colin," I suggested, "would you take me
out to the exhibition grounds to see the flying? Mr. McNair can't go with me," I
added, quickly to forestall the suggestion I
saw trembling on his lips.

Even so he did not fully grasp the situation,
and was about to protest when I glared at him
and he subsided into silence, while Colin
awkwardly consented to be my squire.

"Why wouldn't you let me go to the
show?" McNair asked when we had parted
from Colin and were on our way to my place.

"Because people get acquainted in twos,
not in threes," I replied, "and I want you to
be good and leave me alone to woo your boy
in my own way."

"Very well," he agreed quietly.

"And, McNair," I added, "you're to give

the lad plenty of money to pay his way and
mine, for I want him to feel he is taking care
of me that day."

" Do you, indeed ! " he exclaimed in a tone
of assumed indignation. " You make nothing
at all of ordering a man to stay at home and
pay the bills."

He did not refer to the matter again until
we were saying good-night at the gate, an
hour or two later. As we shook hands he
looked down at me with a twinkle in his eye
and asked, " Must I make allowance for an
ice-cream cone, too? "

" Surely," I agreed, laughing.

He pressed my hand very gently : " I'm
thinking you are wonderfully wise in the weak-
nesses of we men folk, and the way you exploit
them is scandalous."

*   *   *   *   *

So Colin and I went to the pageant, and he
paid my way everywhere, for McNair had
been more than liberal. I could see that he
was proud to be able to ask me to go into
whatever booth took our fancy.

" Now, Miss Dey, let's go up to the grandstand and see the flying," he suggested, as we
came away from having our fortunes told.

I agreed, and we watched, from the best of

seats, the thrilling performance, and every
little while Colin would exclaim, " Did you
see that now, Miss Dey? "

When it was over, and some other phase of
the pageant had begun, I rose and said to
Colin, " Come along, laddie," and he came
along but mutinously, looking very glum as
we made our way down from the grandstand
and along the fence.

When we were a little way out of the crowd
I stopped and explained : " I've an appoint-
ment to interview the aviator, Colin, and I
thought you might like to meet him."

Such a look of awed gladness flashed into
his face that I was more than repaid for all
the trouble it had cost me to make the
arrangement. And, anyway, wasn't he
McNair's boy, and didn't we have to be
friends?

The aviator was a pleasant young chap, and
finding that Colin asked intelligent questions
he answered him man to man fashion, and
allowed him to sit in the machine and showed
him how it worked.

I think I never saw a boy so happy. All the
way home his face wore a rapt expression, as
if he found life too wonderful to be true.
When he left me at my gate, and I thanked

him for a delightful afternoon, he said, with
boyish frankness, " Thank ye, too, Miss Dey,
for introducing me to the flying man. Won't
the kids at school be jealous, though? "

*   .*   *   *   *

So the ice was broken and Colin came with
McNair to tea the next Sunday night and all
the Sunday nights that followed. He would
take a book, throw himself into a chair, with
his legs dangling over the arm, and read.

One Sunday evening McNair came solemnly
in from the garden seat under the maple tree
by the gate, and asked, " May I send the boy
to help wash up? " He had helped me himself once, but he did it so badly that I ordered
him off to his pipe.

" You may not," I answered firmly.

" I thought as much," he growled at me
between puffs.   " It's terrible the way you
bully me, young woman, even about my own
lad."   And he marched slowly back, with his
heavy echoless tread, to the garden seat, where
I usually joined him when I had finished my
work.

But it occurred to me that perhaps Colin
felt left out, so this evening I went in to my
sitting room, where he was draped loosely

over the big stuffed chair I had bought since
McNair became a regular visitor.

My heart was touched at the thought that
this boy had never known any mothering,
though, to be sure, the affection between him
and McNair was the most beautiful thing I
had ever seen in my life. Still they were both
Scotch, poor things, and something told me
the lad needed mothering. I perched on the
arm of the chair and began to talk to him
about " The Three Guardsmen," which he
was reading." From that I went on to lay
my hand on his head and run my fingers
through his hair.

" What are you doing there? " he asked,
turning his head back and looking up at me
with his bright brown eyes. The words
sounded cross, but there was something in the
tone which encouraged me to continue.

" I was pretending you were my little
brother," I answered, and I told him about
Barry.

There are few things more touching than
the way a young person responds to a simple,
sincere confidence given without condescen-
sion.

" Gee, you must have felt awful bad when
he died," he said, sympathetically, and leaned

his head without reserve against my shoulder.
I stooped and pressed my lips very gently to
his forehead. From that moment I began to
love Colin for his own sake, and not because
he was McNair's laddie. He must have felt
the difference, I imagine, for he permitted me
after this to mother him in secret to my
heart's content. The next Sunday night he
came and offered to help me with the dishes,
and we had long talks about things, not important enough to be set down here. Altogether we three were so happy that I might
have known it could not last.

CHAPTER XVII.

THE QUARREL.

McNair and I quarrelled. It happened this way. Our suffrage organisation had decided to have a parade to awaken a slothful public to the importance of our propaganda. I cannot convey any idea of how distasteful the thing was to me; of how I shrank from the unpleasant conspicuousness of walking down a street lined with spectators. We were to be dressed in white and to wear large orange sashes across our shoulders bearing the legend, " Votes for Women."

On a certain evening, a week before the parade, I was contemplating, with a feeling of nausea of which I was deeply ashamed, this outfit lying over the back of a chair, when McNair came in.

" What trumpery is this? " he inquired, superciliously, noticing it almost immediately, and grasping the significance of it as promptly.

I told him that it was my costume for the parade, and because I hated it so much and was so ashamed of myself for my self-consciousness, I was sharper and firmer than I had any need to be.

" You're not going to make a spectacle of yourself like that, are you? " he interrogated contemptuously.

" It all depends upon what one calls a spectacle," I retorted, beating my toe angrily upon the floor.

" I should certainly not permit my wife, if I had one, to carry on that way," he declared threateningly.

" I should certainly not permit my husband, if I had one, to substitute his conscience for mine," I snapped back.

" It's disgustingly unwomanly," McNair insisted.

I felt that I turned pale. " McNair," I said, in a voice that shook, " I cannot permit you to continue your friendship with an un-womanly woman." With a melodramatic sweep of my hand I indicated that the door was convenient.

McNair rose, a red patch burning in each cheek: " You'll live to rue the day you ordered me out," he prophesied darkly, " and mind, once gone, I'll not come back in a hurry, and you'll be gey lonesome." He stamped out noisily.

And I was lonesome. If I had hated the parade before I hated it doubly now, because it

had been the means of separating me from
McNair. I cannot tell you why I minded that
so much, but the sun seemed not to shine any
more with his old brilliance, and the chorus
of the birds became discordant chirps; and
the great strong free wind, that all spring had
lifted my spirit on wings of happiness, became
only a wind which blew the dust in my teeth
and draped my hair in wisps over my collar;
and my business associates were patently fools,
and it was queer that I had never before
noticed that Winnipeg was such an ugly, dull,
windy city.

So the week dragged by.

The day of the parade began with a shower
in the early morning, but long before noon
the clouds had disappeared, and the wind had
dried the streets. Conditions were perfect,
and a great crowd turned out to watch.

There is something exhilarating in large
numbers of people doing the same thing at
the same time, so that in some ways I did not
mind the parade as much as I had expected.
In others I minded it more. It was rather
jolly at the beginning with much laughing and
calling back and forth as we got into line and
raised our banners, at which the wind tugged
hard. But afterward, when we were march-

ing along between the rows of spectators, and
listening to the sneering remarks the wind
blew to us, and when in the crowd we saw the
faces of men we met every day in business and
they raised eyebrows of unfeigned surprise,
but gave no other sign of recognition, that was
very disagreeable.

I tried not to see the spectators, but a horrid
fascination drew my eyes to the sidewalk
against my will. And there, at a certain busy
corner, stood a man and a boy right at the
edge of the curb. I caught my breath sharply
and steered my eyes straight ahead, but when
we came opposite I turned, against my will,
against all reason, and stole another glance,
and was disconcerted to find McNair staring
straight into my face. He gravely lifted his
hat and Colin waved at me, but with a cool
nod I marched on. Yet because McNair had
lifted his hat the day grew brighter, and the
wind did not bother me as it had done a little
while before.

Presently I was aware that among the boys
who were following us was Colin. He sidled
over and slipped a piece of paper into my
hand and sidled away again.

That paper burned my fingers. It made my
palm itch to open it. I could scarcely wait

while we tramped on block after block, up one
street and down another, but at last the order
was given for dispersal, and I spread out the
crumpled note McNair had scribbled on the
leaf of a note book. It read :

You're looking very bonny in your outfit, and I'm proud of you for sticking to
the thing you believe to be right, though
you're terribly mistaken.

Will you have a bite of dinner with
Colin and me to-night? The lad has
hardly spoken a civil word to me for a
week.

Yours humbly,
McNair.

P.S.—I'll bring along a first-rate wash I
have for sore feet.

McN.

There was no sign of Colin or McNair any-
where about, so I went home and washed and
dressed and waited. About half-past six two
sheepish-looking males came diffidently in the
gate, as I saw around the corner of the blind,
and marched slowly up the steps, uncertain of
their welcome. I had planned that I would be
very cold and distant at first, and had settled
in my mind just how haughty I would be, but
seeing them come shyly up the steps I ran and

threw the door wide open and gave each of them a hand and laughed, in order that I might not weep. It was not good policy, as any coquette will tell you, but I loved McNair past all wisdom.

McNair held my hand in his awkwardly, like a lad who has misbehaved, and would like to have the matter settled on the basis of the least said, soonest mended. When he dropped it he reached down into his pocket and brought out a bottle. " That's that foot wash I mentioned," he said brusquely, and then added in the gentlest tones, " Are you very tired, little woman? "

I had not realised how tired I was until then, but at McNair's tenderness the full consciousness of the fatigue I felt as the result of the long walk after being on my feet all day, rushed in upon me, and I turned and went into my room and sat down in a chair and wept, and wept and wept, a thing I had not done for years.

The two males followed me into the room and shuffled about from one foot to the other, and clucked at me and said "there, there," but I would not be comforted. At last McNair strode over to me, and leaning down, lifted me as if I had been a child and laid me on the couch. " I'll go fetch a doctor," he said, as he propped my head up with a pillow.

I caught his hand, " Don't go," I begged. " All the medicine I need is to have you and Colin back."

He pressed my hand almost fiercely at that; drew his brows together sharply, and his mouth down into deep lines at the corners, and turning his head sideways, stared very hard at the begonia on the bookcase.

" What about supper? " put in the practical Colin.

Mrs. Fleming was entertaining a party of friends, and I would not have her disturbed, but McNair suddenly bethought him of a near-by restaurant and went out to order a meal to be sent in.

As soon as he was gone Colin came over and slipped his arm about me. " You're awful moist," he commented, " an' you're wetting my sleeve enough to give a fellow the rheumatis."

For answer I sat up and hugged him.

" Aw what are you doing? " he asked, but his voice was not forbidding.

CHAPTER XVIII.

A Discovery.

I find it difficult to write about the 6th of June, 1912. Here and there in our lives a day is burned so deeply into the memory that even time cannot sufficiently soften its outlines to make it a subject for quiet unemotional contemplation.

As I look back upon it now the thing that happened that day was not so dreadful, but in those days before the war, when all the cheerful little rills of life trickled leisurely along, it seemed to me to be a catastrophe, and my feeling so made it one.

I remember that day in every little detail. I wakened with a thrill of gladness, as I did every day of that wonderful spring and summer, to the lively marital noises of the sparrows in the maple trees about the house.

Just being alive and in love and seeing the sun streaming in gaily through the window meant happiness. Do people love as blithely, I wonder, in moist, dank climates as we do up in the North, where the hottest day is ushered in by a cool, clear dawn and nearly always fades out into a crisp, chill evening. I doubt it. I know that I found life intoxicating that spring.

And this morning I had an especial occasion for gaiety of spirit. A distinguished party of Old Country journalists was passing through the city, and the local Press folk were making a fête day of it, concluding with a banquet at night to which I was going with McNair. For me to be with McNair always meant happiness in itself.

I smiled contentedly as my eye travelled about the room, resting upon the lacey white things I had laid out to wear, and upon my freshly pressed rose muslin dress, which McNair liked better than anything else I had in the way of dresses.

I sprang light-heartedly out of bed and ran to the window to take a peep at the sparkling dew-drenched world. It was going to be a perfect day for the automobile ride in the afternoon and the tea at the old fort.

I stopped on my way back for a glance at the new peach-colored evening gown hanging in my wardrobe, and then I set about cleaning my white shoes, the one thing I had been too tired to attend to the evening before.

While they dried in the sun I dressed and

was just slipping my silk-stockinged toes into them, when Mrs. Fleming came in with a box of roses McNair had sent me. It doesn't seem possible that a day with such a propitious beginning could end as miserably as this one did.

I remember thinking as I put on my new white panama with the rose scarf that I was looking particularly well, and why not, since love and happiness have a way of their own of touching the cheeks with rouge and the eyes with fire.

It was planned that the Winnipeg people should scatter themselves among the guests, so that having a bland, grey-headed Englishman in tow I did not discover until tea-time that McNair was not of the party at old Fort Garry. The realisation brought a slight chill of disappointment, but I reminded myself that he must have been detained unexpectedly at the office, and I concentrated my social energies upon the old gentleman.

The afternoon passed so pleasantly, and we lingered so long that we had to hurry home in the end to dress for the banquet.

I was humming a gay little tune to myself as I pinned a broach into the bosom of my evening dress, when I heard a loud voice asking

Mrs. Fleming if I was in. It sounded like McNair and yet unlike.

There came a loud rap at the door and I opened it, and McNair came in. I saw at once that his face was flushed, his eyes bright and staring, and although he was in evening dress he had a dishevelled appearance. " Well, are you ready for the spread, little woman? " he asked, in a high-pitched voice.

I had stopped still, arrested by a sick sort of feeling as I raised my small round arms to fasten the pins more securely in the soft roll of red brown hair at the back of my neck. Perhaps it was my bare arms, from which the sleeves had fallen away to the shoulder, that attracted his attention, but he gave me a quick, surprised look, and advancing he laid a heavy hand on my shoulder and breathed a sickening smell of alcohol into my face.

" You're looking very bonny to-night, my girl," he said gaily. " Will you give me——" He stopped short as I recoiled sick at heart that the first suggestion of intimacy between myself and this man, whom I loved, should come about in this way.

He was not too drunk to understand the hurt expression in my face. He had been bending over me with his lips close to mine,

but he straightened up immediately and took
his hand from my shoulder.

"I beg your pardon," he said quickly.
"I'm not quite myself—some friends from the
Old Country in the party."

I was at a loss whether to go to the banquet
or stay at home, but in the hope of being
some restraint I went. We were a little late,
and through some mistake there was only one
place left at the head table, which was for
McNair, who was going to make a speech. I
wanted him to let me sit down quietly at one
of the small tables, but he chose rather to
make a disturbance about it and refused to sit
at the head table at all unless they found a
place for me, which occasioned a general
shuffle and directed the attention of everyone
in the room to us. It was most embarrassing.

I do not remember whether I ate anything
at that banquet. I have no recollection of
who was on the toast list or what they said.
I was so sick with dread of the moment when
McNair should be called upon to speak.

It came at last. He rose, and with a hand
on the back of my chair began such a funny
witty speech that I stared at him increduously.
It was quite a new phase of McNair. I
breathed more freely and began to hope it

would pass off without any unpleasantness, but towards the end he repeated a story that had brought roars of laughter at the beginning, and I saw the company look at each other significantly, and I know that I blushed to the very tips of my ears. A few more slips made his condition patent to everyone in the room, and when he sat down it was evident that the applause he received was tempered by pity or reprobation, according to the mental attitude of the listener.

To my acute discomfort I was obliged to share in this disagreeable publicity. I know that many of the women gave me a pitying look, supposing that I was his wife. It would serve no purpose to tell in greater detail the events of that evening, of how from gaiety McNair subsided into touchiness, and from that to a dull stupor; of how I was obliged to call a cab myself and take him home when the banquet was over; of how I went on home along with a dead weight at my heart, which a few hours earlier had been so light and gay.

I felt that I had come to an end of my happiness.

*　　　*　　　*　　　*　　　*

It is one of the tragedies of life—this trek to Canada of men who even in the gentle, humid,

unexhilarating climate of the Old Country
have developed an unslakable thirst. They
come, poor fellows, in the hope of making a
new start in the new world. To Canada of all
places! To western Canada in particular!
Imagine a man who could get up sufficient in-
tensity of thirst to drink to excess in a climate
where the end of every avenue is draped in
haze; coming for surcease of appetite to these
dry, windy plains where the most distant
object meets the brilliant sky with the sharp-
ness of a silhouette; where the night wears no
other veil than darkness; and where, even in
the hottest July weather the dawn comes trip-
ping over the dewy grass with a tang in her
breath. Yet still they come.

Others of their countrymen come also, but
of such a phlegmatic type that even the elixir
of this buoyant prairie atmosphere cannot stir
them to take two glasses where they ought to
take only one. There is no possibility of
bridging the misunderstanding between this
last type of Old Countryman and the
Canadian. He has been accustomed to live in
a climate where there are families who generation after generation drink in moderation
from youth to the grave. He cannot understand, and has no patience with, the social

odium the people of Canada try to throw over the practice.

It is difficult to explain to him that in every country there is a principle of self-preserva- tion which moves society to discountenance those customs which are a peculiar menace to its existence : that morality is chiefly a matter of humidity and altitude.

It is to this instinct of self-preservation rather than to any high ethical qualities that I attribute the attitude of the people of Canada towards the consumption of alcohol. I do not refer merely to its prohibition, but to the social stigma that as long as I can remember has fallen upon men who were known to be habitual drinkers. In Canada in a very large percentage of cases drinking means drunken- ness and drunkenness means the same thing everywhere—poverty. Therefore in the circle of society in which I was raised men who drank were regarded as ineligible. Many charming young girls married them, but their friends looked on with fear and trembling, and saw the wash-tub as a means of livelihood threatening them in the distance. Sometimes their fears were realised, sometimes not, but the fear was so general and so deep-seated that I think the number who escaped misery of a greater or lesser degree must have been small.

This explanation has been offered here to try to make clear the attitude of the average Canadian woman, herself a total abstainer, towards the man who drinks. It should be added that I cannot speak for the women of the brothels or of the top layer of society, both of whom I have heard often indulge quite freely, but not having the acquaintance of either I am not in a position to give authentic information.

Myself, I belong to the bourgeoisie, " that almost people," as Victor Hugo calls us, and which at that is a liberal compliment compared with Mr. Bernard Shaw's ardent dispraise of us.

If we had a peasant class in Canada I should elect to belong to that, but we have not. Contradictory as it may sound we have only two classes of society here : a middle class or bourgeoisie and an aristocracy of wealth.

It is true that some of our rich people have acquired titles, so many, in fact, and frequently for such peculiar services to their country that it has begun to seem to the people of Canada, that is, to the confirmed bourgeoisie, that the British Government would do well to follow the example of the diamond

merchants. Geologists have said that there
are enough diamonds in the world to make
diamonds as cheap as imitation pearls, but the
merchants keep them off the market and put
a high price on those that are for sale.

Recently a Canadian newspaper said of a
certain public man who has done his utmost
to corrupt the civic life of his country, that
he would soon be sufficiently disqualified as a
citizen to receive a title. The statement was
an exaggeration, for many admirable Canadians have, very regrettably it seems to me,
accepted this left-over badge of an out-grown
feudal system. But it is a healthy sign that
Canada laughed.

*   *   *   *   *

Without the foregoing explanation of the
attitude of the great middle class of society of
Canada towards the drinking of intoxicating
liquor it would be impossible to make anybody outside of the Dominion comprehend
the misery I experienced the night of the
banquet.

Even so a person brought up with another
background would doubtless think my grief at
finding McNair a drinking man dispropor-
tionate to the offence, for I knew that whether
or no he drank, McNair was the cleanest-

minded, sweetest-natured man I had ever met.
Nevertheless I wept my heart out that night.

For weeks and weeks I had been thinking
of marrying McNair and had looked with in-
dulgent eyes upon his little faults, intending
to break him gently of them later on. And I
had planned pretty surprises for his home-
comings that would make those dear dark
eyes of his lighten up with a pleased tenderness.

Then one day my castle of dreams had fallen
to ruins. Not because McNair had been
drunk once, but because there rushed back
into my mind little things he and Colin had
said which made it clear that he had been
fighting this thing for years and had never
mastered it. I had not understood them at
the time, but their purport now became
obvious.

Ahead loomed poverty and sordidness, perhaps quarrelling and recrimination, from
which my mind shrank away in distaste.
Under the most propitious circumstances
enough bloom is brushed from the romance
by matters of laundry, Easter hats, boiled eggs
and household accounts. Add to this poverty
and uncertainty, and what chance was there
that the beautiful thing between McNair and

myself would survive? It seemed to me that
our love was like a ball of crystal reflecting
our dazzling northern skies. I could not
endure that it should be clouded by mean,
ugly, humiliating poverty and shame.

I wanted so much that I would be ashamed
to set it down here for fear of being thought
unwomanly, that McNair should take me in
his big arms and press his lips against mine,
but I wanted, too, that his eyes should keep
that look of deep manly tenderness with which
he looked at me when he took my little hand
and held it so long and caressingly in his big
one.

Perhaps that was too much to ask of life. At
any rate I felt that I had been denied it. I
could see no way out as I lay there in the dark
and tried vainly to slip from under the weight
of this horrid reality.

CHAPTER XIX.

A Poor Fighter.

It was more than a week before I saw McNair again. Sitting one evening on the bench near the fence, where I was protected from the inquisitive eyes of the passer-by by the high Caragana hedge, I glanced up from my book and saw him standing just inside the gate. It hurt me to see the look of shame and diffidence in his eyes, so I rose quickly and held out both hands to him.

I felt his large hands tremble as he folded them about my little ones. He didn't speak, but after what seemed a long time a tear splashed on my wrist. He dropped my hands abruptly, strode away and stood beside the maple tree. Resting his elbow on a branch and his head on his hand he stared into the slowly deepening twilight.

I sat down on the bench again and waited. Presently I heard his heavy step and the bench creaked beneath his weight, but I did not look up until he reached over and laid his hand on mine.

"Why didn't you upbraid me?" he said, huskily.

" Because I know how hard you've been trying," I answered, looking up pityingly into his troubled grey eyes.

His fingers closed convulsively over mine. " How do you understand so well? " he murmured. " You who go as straight as an arrow to the goal. I thought you would have no patience with weakness. I was even afraid to come back to you—but I was so lonely——" he broke off abruptly and looked at me appealingly, his face drawn down into deep haggard lines.

" It's because I'm a poor fighter myself," I replied. " Yes, I am," I insisted, waving aside his indignant protest. " You don't see the shrinking spirit I drag after me into every conflict. You don't see how uncomfortable I am before the spoken derision of people for whose minds and ideals of life I have no respect. My intelligence rises above it, but there is something in me, a servility whipped into me in my childhood, that makes me almost ashamed of the truth as I see it."

" But you go on fighting? "

" Doggedly, not bravely," I confessed. " You had no idea, I suppose, that the reason I was so angry with you about that suffrage parade was that I wanted to do what you

advised and leave that which I knew ought to
be done to someone else."

McNair looked at me in amazement. "I
see," he said after awhile, and he got up from
the bench and began to walk up and down
with his hands clasped behind his back.
Finally he stopped in front of me.

"Did you ever read Martin Chuzzelwit?"
he said abruptly.

I nodded.

"Then, my dear girl, I submit you are like
Mark Tapley," he went on. "When the
occasion arises you will 'come out strong,'
and when that time comes I give you my word
that I shall not stand between you and the
thing you believe to be right."

Neither of us suspected the strange dark
days that were ahead, nor could we have
guessed how McNair would keep this lightly
given promise.

CHAPTER XX.

Pauline Intervenes.

There had been a big July hailstorm some fifty miles away, and all the day following Winnipegers went about with chattering teeth. The bright midsummer sun did its best, but the cold wind swept in upon us from the hailed region and drove us into doorways while we waited for street cars, and sent us slinking along in the shelter of high buildings.

Pauline having announced her intention of coming to spend the evening with me, I had prepared an open fire, to which she drew up gratefully. She dropped into McNair's chair, stretched her long limbs out, and clasped her hands behind her head.

"Your room smells suspiciously of tobacco smoke, Aleta," she said, turning her head sideways to look at me.

McNair had called in a few minutes before on his way to the office to bring me a book, but that was no affair of Pauline's.

"Maybe I've taken to the weed," I answered evasively. I suspected she had come to advise me about McNair.

"Smells like a certain Scotsman's pipe," she persisted.

I blushed, but said nothing, while I looked very straight at the fire.

"Aleta," I could feel that her eyes were resting upon me disapprovingly, "I think you had better be careful, dear," she said gently. "He is a very charming man, and you might learn to care more for him than was good for your peace of mind."

Just as if our affections were open to advice! But Pauline is like that. She will fall in love with a judge or the head of a great corporation, and he will be a man of exemplary habits and a pillar of the church, not that the two necessarily go together, but they will in Pauline's husband.

I looked at her as she leaned back in the chair; at her tailored skirt, made by a man, whose label the vain wearer finds ways of displaying to envious feminine eyes, and at her smartly tailored blouse, and I thought how efficient she was. She would never have been foolish enough to fall in love with a man at first sight, without knowing anything about him, and whether he was a proper person to be loved.

As I continued silent, Pauline resumed her

role of Providence deciding my destiny for me.

" That night at the banquet——"

" Pauline," I interrupted her quietly, " you have no occasion to worry about McNair and me; but, if you please, we will not discuss his faults."

I think I must have spoken with some firmness, for Pauline subsided immediately. She removed a bone pin from her dark roll of hair to cover a certain embarrassment.

To atone for my seeming rudeness to a guest I asked hastily : " How is your washerwoman getting along, Pauline? "

" It's a very sad case," she replied, and she related with much feeling the story of Mrs. Jackson's woes.

" Your stories amaze me," I said, when she had finished. " Every case of poverty, except that with which you come personally in contact is due to stubbornness on the part of the poor, and you will fight to the last ditch against any measures that are proposed to eliminate the causes of misery, and yet you get all worked up about the fruits of the system you are upholding whenever it invades your backyard."

" And you Radicals amaze me," Pauline

aptly retorted. " You make a deafening row about the poor, and yet when you come across a case like that of Mrs. Jackson you just make a fresh onslaught on the system and leave her and her bairns to starve. To parody Mr. Dooley, ' God help the poor when they fall into the hands of their friends.' "

I laughed and got up and sat on the arm of Pauline's chair, and slipped my arm about her neck and kissed her.

Pauline smiled.

" Very likely the world needs all the different types of human beings or we wouldn't be here," I said, and we began to gossip about local affairs and forgot our differences.

CHAPTER XXI.

THE CHURCH.

"Would you like to come to church with me this morning? McNair asked, appearing unexpectedly before me, where I sat on the garden seat in the pleasant quiet of a sunny Sabbath morning.

He was dressed in a new brown suit of tweeds, and was looking so fine that it was difficult to refuse him anything; nevertheless I answered firmly, "Indeed I will not."

McNair reached down into the pockets of his coat, brought out his pipe, struck a match on the sole of his tan shoe, lit the pipe and puffed awhile in silence.

I moved over and he sat down, creakingly, on the end of the bench. He took his pipe out of his mouth, blew the smoke up towards the bright blue sky, turned and laid his long arm along the back of the seat, and looked at me gravely.

"We haven't spoken much about religion. You're not an atheist, are you?" he asked, anxiously.

He looked relieved when I answered, "Not even an Agnostic."

" There was a time," I went on, " when I had disposed of the soul, but I began to study history and my faith in a spiritual world came back to me."

McNair looked interested. " How is that? " he inquired.

" I found that all down the centuries the world has produced great men and women who have had a light within; people who have said to their persecutors, and they were always persecuted, ' Do with this physical body of mine what you will; I see life the way I have said and I will not lie about it to please you.'

" The fact that a few great beings have lived who have defied their own bodies and the whole physical world by which they were surrounded would, I think, be strong evidence of a soul, but we have the added fact that the tortures to which they are subjected by a baffled and enraged physical world, instead of driving men away from their ideas, draws the spiritually minded to them. So I have come to believe again that there is probably a soul, and if a soul, why not a God? "

" Then what is your objection to the Church? " McNair asked in surprise.

" The fact that the Church has been one of the most ardent persecutors of these supremely

great souls who have dared to follow the light.
Founded by a rebel and an outcast from
society, a despised soap-box orator, it has
become the leading hound in the pack of social
tyrannies with which to try to drive the fine
free souls of men to uniformity of thought."

" Do you know what I think of God? " I
continued, explosively, for McNair had happened to touch a point where I felt very
intensely.

He shook his head helplessly.

" I think God is a democrat, the only democrat, in fact.   He has filled the world with
human beings no two of whom are alike, and
I think, indeed, I am sure, He meant them to
be left free to develop their differences and to
report of life as they saw it, and He knew that
human nature was so good and clean at heart
that only the beautiful would survive.

" But, unfortunately, there have arisen certain madmen who think themselves gods ; men
who say by their conduct ' I am made on a
special last, different from the rest of my
fellowmen. Therefore, I will set myself up as
a judge of the drawings other men make of
life, and I will rub out those that displease me
lest others not so wise and god-like as myself
might see them and come to harm thereby.'

" So they have gone ruthlessly about in the
world of art, science, literature and politics,
wiping out the lovely things that grow out of
unusual minds. They may have erased a few
ugly pictures, which would have faded of
themselves, for it is a proven fact that no
merely obscene play or book ever lives, but
they have done their utmost to destroy the
warmth, fragrance and beauty of life."

" But about the Church? " McNair put in
mildly, in an attempt to bring me back to the
original issue.

" Well," I said, more quietly, " many of
these self-elected supermen have operated in
and through the Church, and the Church, as
an institution, has promoted their activities.
It is an interesting fact that the Church which
has made the greatest contribution to human
freedom is the one which is conducted demo-
cratically with no preachers to act as middle-
men between folk and their God."

McNair sat thoughtful for some time; puff,
puff, puffing away at his pipe.

" I think you're not very consistent," he
said at last. " When I have pointed out to
you the faults of some of the advocates of
your suffrage cause, you have answered that an
organisation must not be condemned because

some of the people who belong to it are prone to err. Doesn't that apply to the Church also?"

" I don't think so," I answered, " because with the Church it's the other way about. Both in the clergy and the laity there have been magnificent individuals, but as an institution it has been almost unfailingly on the side of despotism and persecution. The Church has not seen, any more than the avowed materialists, that an idea cannot be conquered by prisons or death sentences, but only with another idea bigger and finer than itself. That is the one great outstanding fact written in letters of blood and fire across the page of history, but the world seems to be blind."

We fell into a thoughtful silence, which I broke by rising and saying coaxingly : " In the meantime, McNair, while the world is waiting for us to point out these tremendous truths in it, let us go out to the prairie and pick orange lilies."

" Run along and get your bonnet then," he said, smiling at me indulgently.

We walked along for sometime in silence. Presently I laid my hand lightly on his arm : " Sometimes I've wondered if our friendship

was not a mistake," I said timidly. "We look
at life so differently."

McNair seemed not to hear. He merely
took his pipe from his mouth and pointed the
amber stem at the horizon, where great soft
white cloud domes were piling themselves one
upon another.

"There'll be rain before night," he
remarked.

But later, when we were out on the open
prairie and I had gathered my arm full of
orange lilies, he laid his hand on my shoulder,
"Promise me," he said, and there was a queer
look in his eyes, "that you will never say that
again."

"Say what?" I asked in surprise.

"That our friendship is a mistake. To me,
at least, it is the most precious experience this
niggardly old world has given me."

I was at a loss for a reply, but was saved the
necessity of making one, for he looked down
at my feet and said indignantly, "Woman,
you are trampling on a lily."

CHAPTER XXII.

THE BROKEN SPELL.

It would be pleasant if I could relate that my friendship immediately saved McNair from his weakness, but it did not. After that first outbreak he did not touch a drop for five weeks, and then came a week when he did not draw a sober breath, and when Colin and I were most unhappy.

He was very haughty and defiant of my disapproval when the passion for liquor was upon him; and deeply penitent and touchingly grateful for my continued friendship when it was over. Indeed, that was pretty well the history of the two years that followed.

"I don't deserve your friendship, little woman," he said, one day when he dropped into my office, "but I need it. Take away from a man the one chance more to make good—and then what?"

"Never mind the answer, McNair," I replied, "as long as we both live I shall be your friend, and I'll argue with you and argue with you to your heart's content."

"If the flimsy ground you have for your

outlandish opinions can be called argument,"
he retorted, grinning at me.

" Let's see what you have in your page this
week," he said, taking the proof from under
my hand.

I watched his glance travel over the sheet.
All at once he stopped, and began to read
carefully. His breath came in short pants of
indignation. His face grew crimson and his
eyes glaring.

" Rot . . . . damnable . . . . liar," he exploded at intervals.

Finally he crushed the proof into a ball and
threw it to the far side of the room.

" Is the woman who wrote that letter within
walking distance? " he inquired hoarsely.

" The author was a member of your own
fair sex, sir."

" The scoundrel ! If ever I lay my hands
on him I'll thrash him within an inch of his
life."

" And you'll not prove him wrong by that
method," I replied.

" But why print such a crude, insulting
thing? Couldn't you get anything else to fill
up your space? "

" Nothing," I answered, " that would be

much good propaganda for the suffrage cause."

"I don't see that," McNair growled. "What has this virulent attack on you to do with it?"

"Breeds confidence, and gives people a sense of security. I have always thought there was no greater flash of genius in the Bible than that sentence : 'And ye shall know the truth, and the truth shall make you free.'"

"That's a beautiful theory," McNair retorted, "but this fellow has abused his freedom."

"And greatly helped our cause thereby."

"Mind you this, McNair," I said, shaking my finger under his nose, "there is no cause but a bad one which thrives on the suppression of argument."

McNair caught my hand in his and held it firmly, and he looked long and tenderly into my eyes, so that I forgot about feminism and democracy, and remembered only that my hand lay in the clasp of the man I loved.

A flood of colour surged over my face and neck, and I trembled like a leaf.

At that a great light leaped into McNair's eyes, and he leaned toward me so that I could feel his breath warm on my cheek.

There came a loud rap at the door.

" What is it? " I asked sharply.

" Telephone," sang out the girl on the other side of the partition as casually as if she had not interrupted one of the great moments of a person's life.

The spell was broken.

To this day the sight of that girl's bleached hair and alabaster nose is distasteful to me.

CHAPTER XXIII.

McNair's Story.

My first shock of disappointment at finding McNair a drinking man subsided and I began to persuade myself that if I married him he would give it up for my sake and for the sake of the children with which I hoped our union would be blessed. I was very anxious to believe that. I refused to think of the many cases I had known of the women who had married men to reform them and failed. I could think of only two who had succeeded. Everything I could find about building up the health to resist the drink habit I read, and began to hope that if I gave an intelligent scientific study to the question great things might be accomplished.

Even when McNair came to me one evening red-eyed, flushed and half-dazed with the headache I was not daunted. I made him lie down on the couch and brought a big basin of ice water and bathed his head until the fiery heat had subsided.

" That will do, thank you," he said at last, " my head is much better."

I crossed over to the tea table and brought a cup of strong coffee I had brewing.

His hand shook so as he held it out that I drew the cup away and raised it with my own hand to his lips.

He drank the coffee down quickly, wiped his lips and touched my hand with them. "It's a very precious little hand," he said, smiling.

I did not reply and he looked at me quickly, so quickly that he caught the expression the touch of his lips on my hand had brought to my face.

We were both embarrassed. His face grew grave, and he sat shading his eyes with his hand. At last he sat up straight and took a long breath.

"Tell me, little woman," he asked anxiously, "would you ever forgive a person who had deceived you about something very important?"

"That would depend upon what it was," I answered, with a miserable foreboding of disaster.

"Supposing it was——"

"Oh, please tell me what it is," I broke in, unable to bear the suspense any longer.

His hand shook as he moved it uneasily up

and down the lapel of his coat. "Very well,"
he blurted out, "I had no right to take your
friendship without telling you that I am not
placed like other men that—that—in fact, I am
a married man."

I rose hastily and walked away, hoping to
conceal the blow this was to me. Feeling
dizzy I stopped with my arm resting on the
bookcase to steady myself. I have no idea
how long I stood there, but I was conscious of
McNair coming to me and taking my hand
and leading me to a chair.

He began speaking to me in a quiet, gentle
voice. "I want to tell you the whole story,
if you will listen to me. Many times I have
wanted to tell you, but there is something you
won't understand, and it is that one may have
been so hurt by some experience of one's life
that to speak of it is like putting a knife into
an open sore.

"I think I told you I was turned out on the
world alone at fourteen when my mother died.
Before that, with having to add enough to her
little pension to keep us living, and take care
of her at nights, and learn the lesson she set me
I had no time to run the streets and learn the
things some boys do about life. After she
went I did as she asked me to, worked in the

day time and went to night school, so that I
lived quite apart from other young people in
a dream world of my own, with the memory
of my mother as the one beautiful thing upon
which I looked back.

" I worked in a tailor shop in the day-time
and went to night school until I was between
seventeen and eighteen, when I took a clerical
position at which I hoped to make enough to
put myself through college. Then one night
I went to a cheap variety show and there I saw
the girl and became infatuated with her. She
was a singer and dancer, and I thought her the
most beautiful creature I had ever seen in my
life. In my inexperience I assumed that she
was as good as she was beautiful." McNair
shuddered suggestively.

" Well, to make a long story short I was
married to her a week later." He covered his
face with his hands. " She was a terrible
woman," he went on at last, taking his hands
away, and turning a grey face towards me.
" She was unclean as you cannot conceive of
the meaning of that word. She—she was——"
He broke off and began to walk up and down
with his hands clenched until the tips of his
fingers were white. " I cannot tell you what
she was," he continued, " but after two

months I came home one night to find that
she had taken everything of value in the place
and gone off with another man, and left a
coarse, insulting note informing me of the
fact."

" But if it was as long ago as that you must
be free by now," I suggested diffidently.

He shook his head. " Only if you have
reason to believe them dead. She has looked
me up every few years and begged from me,
and it was so hateful to see her that I gave her
something to go away.

" I wonder if you can understand how sensitive I have always been about this. I took to
drink to try to forget it, but it is not a very
sure cure for brooding. I think I would have
foundered altogether had it not been for
Colin's father whom I had met a short time
before, and who, being older, and knowing the
circumstances, took me in hand and made me
brace up. Then he left me Colin, and finally
I came out here and found you. Maybe you
won't understand the temptation it was to
have the friendship of a good woman after
what I had been through and my years of loneliness . . . but I didn't mean to be cruel to
you . . . . I have never thought of myself as
married . . . . though, to be honest, I guess

I would have yielded to the temptation of your friendship, as I have yielded to other temptations, no matter how much married I had been . . . . for I needed you so badly, and wanted so terribly the thing you have brought into my life." He fell silent, and I sat turning what he had told me over in my mind without speaking.

Presently he touched my hand diffidently. "What are you going to do about it?" he asked anxiously.

"Nothing," I answered, roused from my reverie, "unless spoil you more than ever, to make up for those barren years. What did you suppose I'd do?"

McNair sat blinking at me in amazement. "You are the most astounding woman," he exclaimed. "In big things like this, where I expect you to go up in the air, you are so quiet and reasonable, and then again you'll threaten to break off our friendship over some silly thing, like the other night when I said I didn't see anything the matter with McDonald telling his wife not to go to a certain show."

"It's your sense of proportion that's wrong, McNair. Your having made a mistaken marriage when you were a boy is not a serious matter and can be repaired, but for one person to act as the proprietor of another is a crime. It is a local expression of all the intolerable tyranny in the world."

McNair threw up his hands. " All right, I agree, only don't give me a lecture on feminism to-night, for I am not in proper fighting trim. I'm prepared to surrender to you unconditionally. You stand by a fellow so in tight places. I—I never knew women were like that. Even my mother would fall down on big things sometimes."

I laid my little hand on his arm. " Why didn't you tell me months ago. You would have been so much happier if you had."

He took my hand in his. " I'm having some detectives in the Old County try to find her," he said, ignoring my spoken question and answering my thoughts, and I hope to get clear of the thing before long. In the meantime if you'll give me the benefit of your friendship, as you have in the past, I'll be grateful."

We left it at that, afraid of ourselves, perhaps, if we broke down the barrier of reserve between us, and hoping that our lips would soon be unsealed. But two years crept away and the Old Country detectives whom McNair had employed, found no trace of the woman

In the small personal city in which we lived,
and with our up-bringing, any other than a
legal union was impossible. Sometimes I
thought of it, but I never hinted it to McNair
nor he to me.

CHAPTER XXIV.

WAR.

Then the war came. It burst like a cloud upon our holidaying world, and set us all a-tremble and a-thrill.

Germany had broken the peace of the world and plunged us into night. Very well, we would collect a few Canadians and send them over and they would settle the matter in a few months and come home, and we would give them a banquet, and allow them to die in the poor-house, as had been done to the heroes of other wars.

What days those were! An extra every half-hour! War maps in every hand! A half mile towards Paris—gloom for two days! A great ship sunk—gloom for a week! Our hearts were sensitive to suffering then and the death of a hundred thousand men meant something to us. The blood reeked in our nostrils.

Yet for all that we women, old men and cripples, how we did shout our patriotism from the housetops, so that nobody should miss our voice in the great songs.

What days those were!

The even tramp of troops along the streets!
The morning call of the bugle! The thrill of
an hourly excitement! The awful torment
of soul as one read of rivers full of dead
bodies. Human bodies! It broke our hearts
to read of men with their legs and arms blown
off; with their faces shattered to pieces; men
who would go on living under the most
horrible physical limitations. That was early
in the war before we had grown callous to
the pain of other human beings.

And yet, mixed with our horror, there was a
thrill, a feeling that something had really happened in our time.

What days those were!

CHAPTER XXV.

Then it Came Home.

One evening in October, McNair, whose recent conduct had been discouraging, came to see me. We talked about many things, and when the evening was well advanced, and I was making him a cup of chocolate, he announced, in the droll spectacular way men have, " I've enlisted," just as casually as if he had not been thinking of it the whole evening.

I was dumbfounded. " McNair ! " was all I could find breath to say, as I paused with the sugar tongs poised in the air.

McNair looked modestly heroic, and I felt— I cannot tell you how I felt. Glad that he was not afraid to face physical danger; afraid of that danger for him; sick at heart at the thought that we were to be parted; appalled at the possibility that the parting might be for ever.

McNair was full of the new life and had high hopes that in the change he would find the remedy for his besetting weakness. I had my doubts of war as a reformatory, but I kept them to myself. There are times when the

doubter is intolerable, and I knew that this
was one of them.

Moreover, I had a very strange conviction
about McNair, that some day he would square
away. The coming of this conviction was the
only thing approaching a psychic experience I
ever had in my life.

I was sitting in my room one night worrying about McNair, when all at once it seemed
as if someone had said, " Don't worry; he is
going to give it up." Immediately I had a
sense of the most utter peace. The impression
was so vivid that I wrote a note to him at
once and told him of it.

He was very deeply touched. I suppose I
wrote very convincingly under the impulse of
that spiritual uplift, for I received a very beautiful letter in reply.

I don't think he gave a thought to the super-
natural suggestion, but he was intensely appre-
ciative of my faith in him and my concern for
his welfare.

After that I went about looking resentfully
at all the able-bodied men I met, whom I felt
had as much right to go as McNair. That is
the first of the many internal hates war breeds;
the first of a whole army of ugly, primitive,
degrading emotions, which tend to drag

humanity back to barbarism.   It seemed to me, too, that babies sprang up like toadstools in the homes of young married couples, and that with each new baby the young man added a louder and fresher note to the chorus of patriotism.

The suspicion that these little folks were a war risk insurance may have grown out of the ill-thinking of my own mind, and the idea that the young man grew more noisy as his personal safety increased may have been the fruit of a diseased imagination. I know that there is no more unprofitable occupation than assigning motives for other people's conduct. Each one of us has one great task sufficient to absorb all our energies if we performed it creditably, which is to bring the average of our conduct up so that our own best moments may not be used against us as an evidence of hypocrisy.

But my heart was very sore at the thought of losing the dear man about whom the dreams of my life centred, and my anxiety bred in me a hysteria of fear and hate.

To relieve my mind I plunged into Red Cross work, and one Saturday afternoon at one of the sewing circles, a woman, whom I had always regarded as a very mild and reason-

able person, said, in answer to a lament about
the air raids, " Those German swine will all
have to be killed off." In and out went the
needles.

" Yes, indeed," sighed the fat little lady
near the door, who sat with her toes braced
against the floor, because she was too short for
her chair and had need of a lap, " indeed they
will. They killed me nevvy last week. It's
just awful the things they do."

" And the lies they tell," put in Pauline,
" you can't believe a word of their reports."

A little silver-haired old lady threaded her
needle, and then, sticking it in the bosom of
her dress, looked up at Pauline. " I've
thought sometimes, my dear," she said mildly,
" that our own reports are a little biased. I
noticed this morning that we had re-taken a
town that the reports had not mentioned was
lost."

An awful silence fell upon the room; a
silence full of electricity.

When I looked up Pauline had fixed the
silver-haired lady with a glaring eye. " Do
you mean to insinuate, Mrs. Mayhew, that the
British government would say anything that
isn't true."

The silver-haired lady blushed, under the

cold regard of the meeting, and retracted the insinuation without reservation or equivocation.

"As I was saying," resumed the first speaker, "the Germans have got to be crushed." Everybody agreed that they had.

It was in the early days of the war before the editorial writers, those dauntless heroes of the swivel chair, had transferred the crushing from the German nation to German militarism.

CHAPTER XXVI.

NED IN DIFFICULTIES.

During the two years and more that I had become intimate with McNair I had seen very little of Ned Grant, so that I was rather surprised to get a telephone message from him one evening asking me if he might come over to see me. When he came he was very quiet and abstracted, and I knew that he had something on his mind.

He had been sitting for some time in his customary position of thought, with his hands clasped between his knees, when he looked up at me abruptly and said, " I guess we don't grow up much, Aleta? "

" Who doesn't? " I asked, in surprise.

" We men," he explained, smiling. " Whenever we stub our toes or burn our fingers we run for all we're worth to some woman, on whose sympathy we can rely, for a little petting."

" What particular form do the burnt fingers take this time? " I questioned, touched, as I think a woman always is, by that dependence of a man on her tenderness.

He looked embarrassed. " I can't explain very well—couldn't you pet a fellow in a general way, perhaps, without knowing all the particulars?"

I shook my head in the negative. " No sir, I won't prescribe without knowing the symptoms."

" Maybe you won't do it then, but it's this," he explained. " I was put out of a club to-day to which I have belonged for years, because of my opposition to the war."

I caught my breath sharply. " That was a real burn, wasn't it Ned? "

" It is the most unpleasant experience I have ever had in my life. I resigned, but they wouldn't accept my resignation in order to have the pleasure of expelling me."

" Oh, how mean ! " I exclaimed, indignantly.

" What do you think of the war, anyway, Aleta? " he asked.

I got up and put some more coal on the fire. " I have been trying very hard not to think," I said, as I resumed my seat. " I'd like so much to go with the majority in this one thing—especially— " I broke off, unable to speak of McNair to Ned.

He saw my meaning at once. " Of course,

it would be better for you— " His voice
trailed off into a sigh.

The conservative pictures the man who
opposes authority as a jaunty seeker after the
limelight of publicity, who enjoys being
expelled from clubs and cut dead by old friends
on the street. It is a comfortable way to
think of him, for it makes his persecution a
so much pleasanter matter. The radical at a
distance of either locality or time is apt to
imagine him a great commanding hero. Often,
as a matter of fact, he is a drab medium-sized
man like Ned, discouraged and saddened by
his social isolation, but going doggedly on,
impelled by some unknown law to follow the
stony path of resistance.

To-night he was the very personification of
loneliness and dejection, and my heart was
deeply stirred. I leaned towards him
suddenly. " Listen, Ned," I said, " even
suppose I am not very clear on this thing,
that is no reason why I should not stand by
you and keep you from getting too blue, is
it? "

Ned's face brightened, then darkened.
There would be considerable social odium
involved in being known to be my friend," he
suggested, hesitatingly.

" I don't mind that," I lied, with all the fluency at my command. There has never been a time when I did not mind social odium, but one cannot be altogether a cad. So I made Ned promise to look me up whenever the way became too hard.

CHAPTER XXVII.

COLIN IN A FURY.

One afternoon Colin came dashing into my office, slammed the door after him, threw his cap on my typewriter table, and stood glaring at me, his eyes blazing and his hair standing out every way.

" McNair's a fool," he shouted, furiously.

I nodded and motioned him to a chair, which he did not take. He stood awkwardly before me, his lips working and his fist clenching and unclenching.

" And I'm going to leave him," he exploded further.

I moved the chair toward him with the toe of my shoe. " Tell me about it, Colin," I encouraged him.

He dropped on to the chair and sat there tense, with a hand on each knee, and leaned toward me belligerently.

" Well? " I asked.

He licked his lips, blushed, and began. " Well, it was like this, McNair overtook Jenny Daly and me coming home from a picture show last night, and what does he do but come along with us and begin to talk smart."

" Talk smart," I repeated.

" Yes; silly stuff about I'd got old enough to kiss girls, and first thing he knew I'd be wanting to get married. You know."

I knew that Colin was keeping something back, so I looked him straight in the eye and said " And? "

Colin shuffled his feet.   " There's half-a-dozen of us young folks that go to the show together, and Jenny told the others I'd been blabbing—and—they dropped me to-day—and it's all McNair's fault."

I thought it over a little. " Colin," I said at last, " McNair did act unwisely, but he can't get it into his head that you're a man. He thinks you are still a little boy."

That word man went a long way to appease Colin's wrath.

" It's time he did then," he said, still indignantly, but with subsiding rage. " It isn't as if he hadn't kissed plenty of girls himself."

I was thunderstruck. " What's that you say, Colin? " I asked, quickly.

Colin, who had picked up his cap again, twirled it in his hands. " Well, I saw him once, in Edinburgh, when he was half seas over, kiss the chambermaid in the hotel where we were staying, and likely he has kissed plenty more."

I gave a relieved laugh; I was not much afraid of the competition of chambermaids.

I drew my chair close up to Colin's and we had a long talk about things which shall not be set down here, since they are nobody's business but our own.

When we parted at the door Colin said: "It's a good thing for McNair that he had the sense to take up with a woman like you."

And I answered: " Be sure and tell him I want to see him to-night."

I put a fire in the grate that evening, partly because a grate fire always puts McNair in good humour, partly because it is an excellent first aid to difficult conversations.

As it transpired it was not needed for amiability, for McNair was in one of his rare fits of gaiety that evening.

" The little lad told me the woman wanted to see me," he said, smiling, as he divested himself of his overcoat and laid a box of chocolates on the table.

" That was the first intimation I had of the fact, confirmed later by Colin, that these two

men folk always called me " The Woman "
between them.

" What little lad," I asked, after he had
stretched himself to his full length in his
special easy chair and filled his pipe.

He took his pipe from his mouth; watched
a white curl of smoke ascend toward the ceiling. " Colin, of course," he replied, quite
casually, when the last ring of vapour had disappeared.

I leaned back in my low rocker and clasped
my hands behind my head. " Did it never
strike you, McNair," I asked, " that Colin
isn't a little lad any longer? "

McNair turned to me with a laugh. " I've
a good joke to tell you about that. I caught
the little beggar going home with a girl last
night."

" Yes, and talked so foolishly that Colin
came to me to-day threatening to leave you."

" W-h-a-t? "

Then I told him the whole story, both what
Colin had told me and what he had implied.

" So he had kissed the little sliver," he
laughed, when I had finished.

" Scores of times, no doubt, and they
thought he had been tattling and dropped
him."

McNair chuckled. "The little beggar's beginning young enough. Good thing they dropped him though."

"McNair," I said, looking hard at the fire, "I want to say something to you."

"Say on," McNair replied, in a light tone that made my task more difficult.

"I think you ought to have a talk with Colin," I said.

"What about?" he inquired, casually.

"About all those things which a father would rather tell his son than have him find them out from other boys," I answered.

McNair gave me a quick surprised look as he rose and laid his pipe on the table.

"You're all the father he has," I added, as he began tramping up and down the room, with his hands clasped behind his back.

On one of his rounds of the room he stopped behind my chair, and, laying his hand on my head, he turned my face back so that he could look down into my eyes.

"The boy needs a mother," he said, with a meaning smile.

"Which boy?" I asked, impertinently.

It was an unhappy speech, for his face clouded. "Both of us," he answered. "If only it were possible." And he turned away and commenced his walk again.

Later I felt a very light touch on my head once more, and I might have thought that also was his hand if the mirror above my little mantel had not registered the truth more accurately than my sense of touch.

CHAPTER XXVIII.

FAREWELL.

McNair was sitting in the big chair, smoking in silence, as he had sat ever since he came in.

"Are you quite well?" I asked at last.

He started. "Certainly; why?" he inquired, in surprise.

"You've been here twenty minutes by the clock, and you haven't started an argument yet."

He turned to me with a smile. "We're not going to argue to-night, little woman," he said, with a peculiar inflection in his voice. "This may be our last night together for some time."

I gripped the arm of my chair and bit my lip till it bled.

"I am going to camp to-morrow," he went on. "I might get leave to come back for a week-end, but in case I don't there are some things we must talk over."

Still I could not speak.

He leaned over and took my hand, and we sat thus in silence, while the ebony clock on the mantel ticked away our precious minutes.

" I'm going to leave you Colin," he said at last. " He'll be our boy for the period of the war—and perhaps—if I come back—I'll be a free man and a decent one— " He broke off completely, dropped my hand, rose, and began to walk up and down the room, gnawing his short military moustache fiercely.

That " if " made me sick at heart, but I looked at McNair as bravely as I could, and said : " McNair, you will come back, and sometime it will be all right—and—and we— " I found it impossible to finish the sentence.

McNair stopped and looked down at me. " Will nothing shake your faith in me? " he asked. "After these last months and the way I've neglected you for weeks at a time."

" I believe I'm incurable," I answered.

McNair laid his hand on the back of my chair and stood smiling at me. " A man ought to be able to put up a good fight with such a cause and such backing."

A shadow fell upon my spirit, and I turned my head away.

At that he came around, moved his chair up close to mine and sat down. Then he leaned over and gently drew away the hand I had placed over my eyes and held it firmly in his own.

"I want you to tell me what's worrying you, little woman," he demanded, quietly.

"I cannot," I replied, resolutely.

"Then you're not playing fair with me," he declared, frowning. "For nearly three years I have unloaded every care of mine on to your shoulders."

I caught my breath sharply. It was so precious to feel such protecting tenderness at hand. Still I resisted it. "This is the one thing," I said, "that I really cannot tell you or I would."

"Then I know," he said. "It's that you don't believe in the righteousness of the war."

I was amazed at his insight. "How did you guess?" I stammered, taken aback.

"Do you remember that Sunday when I wanted you to go to church and you wouldn't?"

I nodded.

McNair went on: "You made it quite clear to me that day that your mind would nearly always register opposition to the accepted thing, not because you wanted it to but because you are constituted that way. When the war came I expected you to fall out with it before long."

I looked at McNair in astonishment too great for words.

" I wanted to know," he concluded, " whether it had happened yet."

" Why? " I asked, quickly.

" Because I wanted to tell you while we were together that nothing like that need ever come between us."

I laid my head against McNair's sleeve and sprinkled tear-drops upon it.

I felt his muscles tighten up. I knew that my head against his arm was a great temptation, and to-night I wanted it to be so. I had thrown discretion to the winds. With two words McNair could have picked me up and carried me off to be his wife in fact at least.

But this night McNair was strong. Tenderness conquered passion, and by and by I felt his big hand laid gently on my head. " There, there," he clucked, like a mother to her child.

" You're such a good man, McNair," I said, with a catch in my breath. And indeed he is one of Nature's noblemen. We must accept

it as her prerogative not to make the rose
without the thorns.

"Yes," McNair agreed candidly with my
remark; "there are plenty worse men, even
though I have my little faults."

He is very susceptible to praise, is McNair,
which is only another way of saying he is a
man.

We fell into silence, which I broke after a
little by saying: "It's a great weight off my
mind.   I have been fighting desperately all
winter to keep my faith in this cause for your
sake, because, at best, it was so hard to have
you go. I don't know how to tell you what
a happiness the last three years have been to
me."

McNair straightened up in his chair
abruptly. "Don't," he said, hoarsely; "you
shouldn't tempt a man too far."

I sat all a-thrill, hoping in my heart of hearts
he would not be able to resist temptation.

The clock ticked along like a railway train
in the quiet of the room while I waited with
bowed head for whatever might happen.

When McNair spoke again it was in a well-
controlled voice of quiet gravity. "Perhaps,
when I come back, I may feel that I have a
right to tell you what they have meant to a

man who had about given up hope. But—
well—what I was going to say is that the
future immediately ahead will be difficult
enough, without adding to our burdens. It
is necessary to my peace of mind to have your
promise that you will share any worry that
may come to you with me."

" But, McNair," I objected.

" Promise me," he said, firmly.

I promised.

* * * * *

McNair went to camp the next day and I
did not see him again before he sailed for
England, as the troop train went through in
the middle of the night.

He wrote me from Kenora. Such a letter!
So full of hope that he would do credit to
Canada and the dear ones left behind, and
that he might be spared to come back to this
glorious country of his adoption and make a
place for himself, but if Fate had other plans
for him he hoped he would die bravely and
so justify my faith in him that way.

Colin, who had taken a room at Mrs.
Fleming's since McNair left, came in as I was
reading it.

I looked up at him. I was not crying.
My heart was bleeding inwardly.

" What's the matter? " he asked.

I opened my mouth to answer, but no sound came. I wet my lips with my tongue. " McNair's gone," I said.

Colin turned a sickly green colour and toppled over. He had been growing very fast lately and was none too strong.

In the effort to revive and comfort the lad I found the only possible ease for my own anguish.

CHAPTER XXIX.

War Profiteers and Soldiers.

It was Sunday afternoon, and Pauline and I were tramping along the dusty road homeward from a long walk, during which, having discussed perfectly innocuous subjects, we had agreed. Unluckily she began to tell me about some investigations that a committee, of which she was a member, had been making into the way the wives of soldiers spent their separation allowances and their time.

" We found Mrs. Thompson was gadding around with other soldiers and Mrs. Davis had bought a new gramophone," she informed me in a low confidential tone; " and of course we explained to them as nicely as we could that they would have to change their ways."

" What business was it of yours? " I inquired, indignantly.

Pauline coloured up. " What do you mean?" she asked, sharply.

" I was just wondering whether you thought the private soldier didn't earn his dollar ten a day by risking his life at his country's behest."

" Of course, but that has nothing to do with it."

"Perhaps not, but I happen to know that one of your committee, who, by the way, is the wife of one of our most successful war profiteers, has two or three young men followers, and another has bought a new limousine in which to go around and advise the wives of soldiers that they ought not to buy gramophones. Has your committee done anything about that?"

Pauline assumed her most bored and supercilious expression. "You make me tired, Aleta," she said; "you don't believe in the war, but you are always professing to be keenly exercised about the wrongs of the private soldier."

"It's not pretending," I said, hotly. "My believing in the necessity of the war has nothing to do with it. The fact is that the country of which I am a citizen has used every means in its power to coerce these men into the army, and then you go prying around into their homes as if they were objects of public charity. You seem to feel that the war profiteer, who makes from two hundred to a thousand per cent. profit out of the rotten supplies he furnishes the army, has earned his money, and, of course, enjoys the good old British privilege of spending it as he pleases, but the soldier, who is only risking his life, has not a quit claim deed to his dollar ten but his family must also relinquish their personal liberty. What people like you want is a bargain in patriotism in which someone else dies and pays and you gloat."

From that it was an easy step to an argument about the war, which lasted fifteen minutes and ended with our being in such a state of mind that we did not either of us want to know the truth unless the truth justified our point of view.

After we had separated with a curt word of farewell I thought that perhaps if I had been more gentle I might have converted her to my point of view. Possibly she thought the same of me. If she did I fancy we were both wrong, for Nature made her to shout " Hear, hear ! " and she made me to shout " No, no ! " The bridge between two such extremes is not arguments but generations.

CHAPTER XXX.

SOCIALISM OR CHRISTIANITY.

" What is the solution, Ned? " I asked, as he tramped up and down the room, his hands pushed deep into his trousers pockets, and poured out a flood of invective against the present social system.

" Socialism," he said, decisively.

I shook my head doubtfully.

" Why, I thought you told me the other day that you were almost converted to socialism," he exclaimed, impatiently. Ned sees such ideas as appeal to him with absolute clearness and he has no patience with shilly-shallying.

" That was the week before last," I objected. Things move so fast these days that I think one ought to be allowed to change one's mind at least every two weeks without being accused of inconsistency."

" Well, what's the matter now? " His tone was sharp, for he is rather touchy on the subject of socialism.

" The matter is that you Socialists have exactly the same sense of values as the

Capitalist. You are looking for the panacea of human misery in material success. The difference is that you want it for the many while the Capitalist wants it for the few."

Ned whirled around and faced me. "What would you suggest as the alternative?" he asked, coldly.

"Perhaps a return to an old ideal of love as the only conquering force in the world, and service—not grabbing—as the one source of human happiness."

He leaned his elbow on the mantel-shelf and glared at me. "Good God, Aleta;" he exclaimed, "do you want to return to that Christianity which has put the people in chains to their masters and women in slavery to their husbands?"

"You are speaking of churchianity," I objected.

"It comes to the same thing," Ned insisted. "Found a new church and inside of fifty years it will have become as much the tool of capitalism and the policeman of authority as is the old one."

"Granted," I said, "but found your socialist commonwealth, and in less than fifty years it will have become a much greater tyranny than our present system. This war

has thrown some light on the treatment
majorities will give minorities when the whole
of society can be organised by the government
for their suppression. Your socialist commonwealth will be a new kind of hell for anyone
who happens to have an original mind."

"Anyway the great mass of the people will
have a chance to live decently and get an
education."

"But they won't be made either good or
happy that way," I remonstrated. "Greed
and fear are the emotions out of which have
grown the present social structure. Whatever
social structure you may erect to-morrow will
be dominated by those two emotions unless
you substitute for them a new idealism of faith
and service."

Ned said, grimly: "Then the situation is
hopeless."

"Sometimes, Ned, on rainy days I think it
is," I agreed. "I am often overwhelmed by
the idea that Nature has moved the western
nations to self-destruction because these great
materialistic imperialistic world powers stood
in the way of a new idealism; that the militant
powers of Europe will annihilate each other
in this war; and in the next the United States
and Japan will complete their self-destruction,

and thus leave the stage clear for the middle
east, the cradle of all the great religions,
except materialism, to lead humanity up to
something higher."

"You remember what the old Hebrew poet
said : 'Behold the nations are as a drop of
a bucket, and are counted as the small dust of
the balance.'"

"It is not a pretty thought," I went on,
"for if that is the case we Pacifists are wrong
in seeking to impede this orgy of destruction.
Perhaps in the interests of posterity we would
be better employed in cheering it on to its
logical conclusion of devastating plagues,
revolution and the consequent disintegration
of these vast empires into little states."

"You are too much alone, Aleta," Ned
said. "You ought to get out and take plenty
of exercise. Those ideas are morbid."

"I know," I answered, "the way to be
happy is to pick out some formula, pin your
faith to it and refuse to think any more. 'The
Germans must be wiped out' is simple and
satisfying, especially if one happens to be a
woman, an elderly man or a cripple. Or if
you have another sort of mind, 'Down with
the capitalist system.' But when one reads
history and sees how often the answered prayer

of yesterday becomes to-morrow's curse it gives one pause."

Ned laughed cheerfully. " Then don't read it," he advised. " No use fussing about the centuries ahead. What the world needs right now is Socialism."

" And the next thing after that Christianity and freedom."

Ned frowned.

*   *   *   *   *

The old prophets promised us a new heaven and a new earth. The spiritualists are giving us a new heaven; the British Labour Party has promised us a new earth, but it seems to me that a more pressing need than either is for a new humanity. Otherwise the new heaven will soon become as exclusive and aristocratic as the old and our new earth a fresh monument to tyranny.

But teach every man behind the plough and in the ditch that he is as much the son of God as the Bishop or the Prime Minister, and knows His will as accurately and you will have broken the degrading spell of reverence which binds men's souls in bondage. You have put him upon a plane where no trumpery medals or titles bestowed upon one man by another can exalt him in his own estimation, and where no indignity at the hands of his fellow men can bend him from his principles, or degrade him in his own eyes. Then will men dream great dreams and tell the world of them " and the eyes of them that see shall not be dim, and the ears of them that hear shall hearken."

CHAPTER XXXI.

McNair's Letters.

Sometimes they were only scraps pencilled on the thin checked leaves of a notebook. Occasionally they were written standing up in a hut that was little better than a sieve, as that position, he remarked, philosophically, exposed the least of his considerable surface to the rainfall. Penmanship suffered in these circumstances, but McNair's letters, fragrant with the smoke of his pipe, were like a charm in bringing me happiness.

In one of mine I had asked whether he would care to stay over there for a while in case peace was declared, and he wrote :

" Would I stay long in Europe if peace ' broke out ' ?   I wouldn't stay any longer than to have a bath and a shave, and maybe I wouldn't wait for those if the boat happened to be in a hurry. One doesn't usually dawdle in a graveyard longer than necessary, especially such a crude one as this will always seem to me."

It seemed to me that some of his descriptions of scenes at the front were peculiarly vivid,

but I own to being so infatuated with McNair
that I am incapable of judging anything of his
dispassionately, so I will set one down here.

" For nearly two weeks we have had nothing
more exciting than an occasional work party
and one march up to the front in the capacity
of reserve. We were not required on that
occasion, so marched back again.

" It was a fearsome march for a while. The
greater part of the horizon looked like the
mouth of a furnace. It was one of those still
nights, without wind, and the whole country
quickly became enveloped in the haze of
spring, mixed with the haze of bursting shells,
and the flame from the guns and explosives
looked more than ordinarily lurid. As our
march led us into what seemed the middle of
it we may possibly have missed some of the
artistic effects, especially when passing through
a ruined town one could hear above the tramp
of many feet, the clatter of many timbers and
hoofs, the crash of shells a few blocks away
and the rattle of falling walls, as the very much
shattered town was being further shattered.

" However, as I have said, we were not
needed, and presently, after midnight, the
strafe eased off a bit, and by the time we got
back to camp day was almost breaking, and

there was only an occasional shot to disturb
the quiet of the morning. The country was
still clothed in its robe of mist — a
fairly close fit — as above it the peculiarly
tufted tops of the trees appeared like little
green islets in a very still sea."

*   *   *   *   *

On one occasion we quarrelled. It was my
fault. I sent him an ultra-feminist story in
which the heroine asserted her independence
of the men of her family in a decidedly force-
ful manner. She was absolutely right, of
course, but my sending the story to McNair
was provocative.

He wrote back that he didn't like the story
(I knew he wouldn't), that the heroine seemed
to him unwomanly and self assertive, and much
more in the same vein.

The letter came when I was suffering from
a bad cold in the head and was a way behind
with my work and exceedingly irritable. It
made me very angry. In the furious white
heat of my indignation I sat down and wrote
him my candid opinion of his outlook upon
life.

It is difficult quarrelling by letter, and
across the ocean at that. Between this out-

pouring of my wrath and the reply to it there came half-a-dozen or more every-day letters.

" I've a notion I got a good wigging in your delightful letter," he wrote; " I am not very bright, but I fancy old-fashioned prejudice keeping an open mind, and similar phrases, heavily underscored, must have had a personal application.

" I hope you won't be more indignant than ever when I tell you that I laughed until I was weak over your epistle and at my glorious escape in not being within reach of you at the moment of writing.

" Go ahead, little woman, and frame a declaration of independence a day, but you won't be independent. Don't you know that people may be more completely bound by their affections than by any legal contract?

" I am sure that if I had consulted my intelligence I would never have chosen you as my friend, but—well—anyway I did, or you chose me, for you began it, of course. At first I had vague plans for making you over. Now the idea of your ever being orthodox moves me to laughter.

" In my old age I am even foolish enough to feel that I shouldn't like the little rebel

to be different. When I had made you over
you would probably be a person of whom I
approved more thoroughly than I do of you,
but you wouldn't be you; and nobody who
was not you could fill the place in my life
that you fill.

" As the chances of losing life increase one
sees many things from a different angle.   I
don't know whether I am making my meaning
very clear. I think what I am trying to say
is that I can't seem to care as much as I used
to about the tools people use, or even the
task itself, as about the spirit in which the
task is undertaken. I think you must feel this
too, otherwise your letters would not be the
great stimulus I find them to carry on in a
task of which you do not approve.

" Don't be cross at me for laughing, will
you? This is a pretty sombre life and it's not
often I have a good chuckle."

*   *   *   *   *

One day there came a letter telling me the
good news that McNair had conquered his
particular weakness for the time being, and,
he hoped, for all time. After that there was
a warmer and more personal note in his letters
which precludes the possibility of exposing

them to strangers' eyes. Although no trace
had as yet been found of his wife he would
soon be legally free, so that we felt the barriers
that had divided us disappearing.

CHAPTER XXXII.
Two Telegrams.

I have no patience with the claim that women pay the biggest price in war. It is a lie. My part was easy compared with McNair's, but it was hard enough.

A ring at the door early in the morning. I started up in bed in a cold sweat—was it a telegram? A telephone call late at night and my heart was in my mouth; called out from a meeting I went white.

A strain such as that slowly wears away one's nervous energy, so that the shock, when it does come, finds one with reduced powers of resistance. And it always comes in the end with the suddenness of a bomb explosion.

It was a windy March day, with a cold grey sky. Dirty ridges of snow on northward-looking lawns glowered up at the dark clouds a defiance of Spring's notice to vacate. The wind, with its subtlety in finding playthings, collected newspapers from the wind alone knows where, and sent them tumbling down the middle of the street or whipped them up and flattened them against a billboard. Then

it would go wailing off around the corner, only
to come tearing back between two high buildings with a handful of grit to throw in one's
teeth. The rawness of it ate into one's very
bones.

It was along about three o'clock in the
afternoon that I heard a voice outside my
door asking for me. There came a rap.

" Come in," I called out carelessly.

It was a telegraph messenger.

I signed the book, took the yellow envelope
and waited until the door had closed upon
him.

It was from the military office at Ottawa.
Lieut. McNair had been gassed and wounded.

I sat down dumb and stricken.

A thousand times I had read gassed and
wounded in the casualty lists, and after the
first few months of terrible sensitiveness I had
grown callous, so that it did not hurt to read
those words.

Now they blazed suddenly into life. They
meant a human being, kind and lovable,
writhing in mortal agony; they meant a man
torn and suffering in a strange land, with a
wide ocean rolling between him and the ones
who loved him best.

It meant McNair fording the waters of

affliction alone—unless—unless—Oh God!—
unless he had died.

I rose, put on my hat and went into the
drear March day to find Colin.

* * * * *

Three days passed in a vain effort to learn
further details. I cannot tell what I suffered
during those days. Hour after hour the rising
fever of misery grew, until, proving in excess
its own anæsthetic, it brought on numbness;
then followed an hour or two of comparative
peace while the exhausted nerves gathered
fresh energy for protest, and again another long
stretch of misery more wearing and exhaust-
ing than the last. So the three days crawled
away. Impotence is the peculiar sting of this
particular form of ordeal, combined with
uncertainty, which gives the tortured imagination free rein to create its own hell of horror.

For three days and nights I traversed the
battlefields of France. I found McNair in
No-Man's-Land, with an arm blown off and
gasping for breath; I dug him out from
beneath a pile of dead bodies, between
trenches, saturated with their blood and his
own, which dribbled from the stub of his
leg. I stumbled upon his half-naked body in

the bottom of a trench, slimy with blood and
crawling with vermin, and I raised him up to
find half of his face was blown away and that
he was stone blind.

I walked alone at twilight over a deserted
battlefield, and as I passed a certain place the
evening breeze blew to me the smell of carrion,
and I turned and looked and there were three
black birds pecking at a long dark thing on
the ground.

Those were the lesser horrors that I dreamed
—the things it is possible to put into words.

*   *   *   *   *

The afternoon of the third day there came
another telegram. I was standing out in the
general office when they brought it to me. I
remember groping my way back to my own
room. I remember that I stood with the ugly
yellow thing in my hand, choking, until it
suddenly came to me that the certainty that
McNair was dead would be easier to bear than
the awful anguish of the past three days.

I opened it.

It was a cablegram from McNair himself
saying that he was in hospital with a thigh
wound and out of danger.

That is all I remember.

When I opened my eyes Pauline was sitting beside my bed. She rose, pushed the hair back from my forehead and kissed me. Pauline never kisses me except when I am in trouble, but then she does it with a beautiful tenderness.

I looked about me. It was night and Pauline had turned off all the light in the room except the electric lamp on the table.

" Where's Colin? " I asked.

" I've sent him to bed," she said. " The poor boy is pretty well upset with the double shock."

" I know," I said. " Both telegrams were a shock."

Pauline smiled. " I meant the worry about his two guardians," she explained.

I opened my eyes in surprise. " Did Colin worry about me? " I exclaimed.

" You seem to have completely bewitched those two Scots," she laughed. " Colin came over for me, looking like a grim ghost, and went about with a strained look that was painful to see until I told him on the word of the doctor and the nurse that you were all right. When they were gone he came down and told me he could look after you himself, but I persuaded him to let me stay.

" Dear old Colin," I said.

Almost at that moment the door was pushed open and Colin came softly in, rubbing his eyes.

Observing that I was awake he crossed over to me with long strides, and stood looking down at me self-consciously. He was a big chap now, of a tall man's stature.

" Well, you're a great one to go fainting all over the place," he scolded me.

Talk about the reserved English. They are a gushing river of sentimentality compared with the Scotch. But I love the shy, dour Scot. I never agree with them, for the ones I know are nearly all double-dyed Tories like Pauline and McNair, but I love them.

CHAPTER XXXIII.

The Struggle.

My collapse at the time McNair was wounded was not due altogether to the shock of that event, but because it came on top of an intense emotional struggle which had been going on within me for weeks. As the fury of the war spirit rose it became more and more difficult for me not to protest against utterances which to my ears sounded brutal in the last degree.

One evening, on my way to a meeting at Labour Temple, I turned a corner suddenly and almost collided with one of the city's best-known Christian laymen, the head of a large corporation, which at the beginning of the war had reduced the wages of its girls from nine to seven dollars a week and made a front page contribution to the patriotic fund.

" You came around that corner like a German bullet," he said, laughing as he righted himself.

" A sad affair, this war," he continued, " but we've got to go on until we've wiped the last German off the earth."

" Not Christian," he chuckled, in answer to my murmured protest. " I'm not so sure about that. Anyway, I've never had any use for this other cheek business. A little hate isn't a bad thing. We must teach our young men to be brave."

He limped away. He has a club foot.

I continued on my way, sick at heart; also angry. It was so easy, I thought, for a man to be brave with other men's lives. But I caught myself up short at that, for I wanted more than anything else not to grow bitter and cynical. So I forced myself to face the fact that possibly the tendency on the part of cripples to glorify war is due to a gnawing regret at their own lack of physical power. What right had I, who was not handicapped in any way, to judge the mental reactions of a person who had borne a burden like that through life? I tried to reason myself into calmness, which was badly needed in the stormy meeting that followed.

A resolution was on the order paper opposing conscription of men until all the wealth of the country had first been conscripted, and as soon as the secretary read it a little fat woman rolled to her feet and demanded shrilly, " Do you mean to say you would take money we have in the bank? "

The secretary assented.

" Then I'm dead agin it," the fat little
woman went on in her high piercing tone.
" I've given my son, and I was perfectly willing to do that, but you're not goin' to touch
my hundred dollars."

Immediately pandemonium broke loose.
People jumped up all over the room and
shouted things at each other, without any
formalities in regard to the chair. The pre-
siding officer banged the table but they paid
no attention to her. It was fifteen minutes
before order was restored, and the motion
was dropped by tacit consent.

A sullen anger burned on like a live coal,
bursting into flame again the moment the
meeting was dismissed. People gathered about
in little knots and began to talk noisily and
excitedly, the object of the talk on both sides
not being to arrive at the truth, but to ram
their opinions down each other's throats.

" I don't see what you Pacifists make such
a fuss about," said a brisk young business
woman, who had come into a high salaried
position when a young man in the firm for
which she worked had enlisted. " Everybody's got to die sooner or later."

I had started to reply when a big, aggressive woman, prominent in our suffrage movement, elbowed her way into the centre of our group and looked about her belligerently. Her eye caught mine.

" Isn't it a disgrace that Congresswoman in the United States voting against war? " she sneered.

" But I thought that in our suffrage campaign you urged that women should be given the vote for that very reason—because they would be opposed to war," I objected.

" I meant that they would be opposed to wars that are past, like the Crimean War or the Boer War, but I never dreamed that women would be opposed to war in their own time or I wouldn't have worked for the vote. The idea ! "

There seemed no use in arguing with a woman who could talk such drivel, but when I got home I felt uneasy about it. Was my silence in all these cases a dignified restraint or the same old spirit of cowardice which had dogged me all my life and made me afraid to differ from the accepted thing? I wished there was some way of being sure.

The following week I was attending a farmers' convention in another city, at which

a speaker pleaded eloquently for conscription.
" Let us have conscription at once, and round
up these slackers who are hanging about the
city pool rooms," he urged.

Applause that shook the rafters.

A young farmer rose and said, in a slow
pleasant voice : " And I move that we farmers
keep out of the profits on our grain only the
private soldier's pay of a dollar ten a day and
give the rest to the government to carry on
the war."

Six scattered handclaps greeted the suggestion, two of the loudest clappers being city
people. There seemed to me something so
sinister in this eagerness to conscript other
people's lives and reluctance to part with their
own dollars that I went to the reception the
Women's Canadian Club was tendering to the
delegates that evening with a bitterness of
spirit toward the war party in my own country
which was no more Christlike than their hatred
of the German people.

I found myself, in the course of the evening,
in a window recess with one of those commanding society women who always intimi-
date me. Having discovered that I was a
Pacifist she levelled her lorgnette at me fear-
somely. " But the atrocities, my dear, the

atrocities," she said. "How can you over-
look them. Surely people who do things like
that ought to be exterminated."

"Well, of course, in the great republic to
the south women are said to have thrown
babies into the fire at East St. Louis, and leading citizens to have burned a man's eyes out
in Tennessee and to have slowly tortured him
to death, but they really didn't mean anything
by it. It was just their democracy breaking
out. In Germany it is their autocracy finding
an outlet, and that makes all the difference
don't you know."

"Now, why bring up the Belgian cruelties
to the Congo natives, and England's flogging
and hanging of Egyptians in the Denshawai
affair. As I remember it those were only
coloured people; also in America. You must
see yourself, young lady, that there is a vast
difference between crucifying a white man and
hanging a coloured one."

"Yes," I said, "I have no doubt their
naked bodies have quite a different effect
against the sky line."

*   *   *   *   *

If the war party had been completely
dominated by this callous, brutal, unimagin-

ative selfishness it would have been a simple
matter to oppose them, but mixed with the
spirit of profiteering, and blood-thirstiness,
and the lust for revenge, and the furious hate
there was great devotion and unselfishness and
the most frightful suffering.

Pauline was passionately sincere in her conviction that if I had my way and peace was
brought about by negotiation the world would
go straight to damnation. She was so certain
of it that she was willing to resort to means
that she knew were wicked to keep me from
having my way. And she was stronger than
I, because she knew that she was infallible and
I did not.

I looked into my own heart day by day and
I tried to simplify the issues, but nothing
was very clear. I asked myself over and over
again whether if I were to go forth and
demand that we should have peace I would
not be assuming the same omniscience that
Pauline assumed in insisting that we must have
war? Could one be sure that Nature had not
found it necessary to destroy the western half
of the world in order to give the power to
some more idealistic people? Might not this
blind stampede of death have a meaning far
beyond the grasp of the present generation?

And then again I would ask myself whether these were not merely excuses for my weakness with which I was trying to soothe my conscience for my inactivity, rather than arguments. Try as I would to analyse my emotions I could not be sure. From these fluctuations of my own mind I came to understand that many of the inconsistencies on the other side were due to similar uncertainties. I began to see that the little fat woman, who clung so greedily to her hundred dollars, had very likely her great days when she would have given not only her son but her hundred dollars and herself also for her country; and the young girl, who was so well satisfied to take the position vacated by a soldier, probably had glorious hours when she would willingly give it up and go scrubbing for a living if she thought it would benefit the cause in which she believed. I saw our souls swinging on pendulums between the earthly and the spiritual worlds, dominated now by one, now by the other.

So I had blundered along for months, sometimes protesting, sometimes letting things pass and often hating the other side with a ferocity which gave the lie to my pacifist convictions, and always I hated myself for hating. Daily

I prayed that if there was a spirtual force that
came to the help of human beings it would
help me to acquire the spirit of love and
mercy and kindness which my mind saw so
clearly were the only irresistible forces in the
world. So I might have muddled along to the
end had not the government begun to forbid
us to discuss the war at all, except favourably.

I found my personal telephone was being
tapped. One day at noon I remembered that
I wanted some information from the military
office about Red Cross Nurses for one of our
readers, so I used my own telephone. The
blur in the sound, which I had noticed for
some weeks, came as usual, and the gentleman
who answered grew very wrath about the
listener.

" There's someone on this line," he
bellowed at me.

I answered sweetly : " Yes, there seems to
be."

" Get off," he roared; " get off this line."
The extra receiver went up with a soft thud.

I could hardly take his message for laughing. But though I laughed there was something in this that bit. I, a Canadian of
Canadians, whose parents and grandparents
had hewed their way in this new harsh country

against great odds; I who had given to its making all of myself that I had to give was being treated as a criminal because I insisted upon discussing the aims for which my countrymen were being asked to die; for which the man I loved lay suffering in England.

A call from the censor warning me that I must say nothing about the proposed conscription measure which would tend to rouse opposition to it if it passed, crystallized my irresolution into action. Since when had Canadians relinquished the right to discuss unmade legislation? Was this Prussia or Canada in which we lived?

Well, anyway, I began to distribute pamphlets demanding that freedom of speech and of the press be preserved, and one day I was arrested and sent to jail.

CHAPTER XXXIV.

GETHSEMANE.

The second night in jail I walked alone in my Gethsemane, and the Devil of Doubt, almost a visible presence, stood at my right hand and jabbered in my ear the whole long night.

"You've made a hideous mistake," he whispered. "You have mistaken egotism for insight."

"You are the one hundred and fifty billionth part of one thread in the cobweb which time is weaving with the countries of the world as the spokes, centuries as the hitching posts, and the whole human race as the binding cord. And you have decided that you don't like the pattern. That is very droll. You, the one hundred and fifty billionth part of one thread have decided to change the design."

"But surely," I answered the fiend, "surely when one is willing to give up friends and freedom and social standing, perhaps even health and life itself, that must prove the righteousness of one's cause."

The fiend chuckled. "Leaving out the loss of friends and social standing, are not the other things being given generously and courageously on the other side, and in vastly greater numbers," he jeered.

I had to admit they were.

"Mark my words," he said, and I could almost hear him lick his lips in the darkness, "all down the centuries the earth has been fertilized with the blood and bones of people who have given their lives freely for ill causes, and Nature has not deviated one hair's-breadth from her purpose to justify their sacrifices. Nor will she for yours. If you're wrong, you're wrong, and if you're right, you're right, and though you died a million deaths you will not alter that."

I sighed, a sigh that came from the very bottom of my heart. "Very well," I said, finally. "I could only follow the gleam as I saw it."

I had peace for a time after that.

*   *   *   *   *

Just as I was about to fall asleep the Fiend came back again.

"Suppose you are right," he said; "what good do you expect to come from your opposition to authority? Don't you know that the one thoroughly congenial pastime of every succeeding generation is the stoning of the prophets? "

" But posterity always raises monuments to the stoned prophets, so they must accomplish something," I objected.

" True," Doubt assented, " but not to their ideals."

" To what then? " I asked.

" To their stubbornness in clinging to their ideals against coercion. The only thing humanity really admires is obstinacy.

" Before Jesus there was Isaiah, that glorious old firebrand of a Hebrew poet, who put the woes of the poor into song, and after Jesus came Karl Marx, and one day a great orator arose in a temple created as a monument to Jesus, the great apostle of the homeless, and introduced a furious attack upon Karl Marx by that passage from Isaiah :

" ' They shall not build and another inhabit ; they shall not plant and another eat ; for as the days of a tree are the days of my people, and mine elect shall long enjoy the works of their hands ! '

" And nobody observed any inconsistency," the fiend concluded, " because Isaiah and Jesus are a long time dead. A great leader serves only his own generation. Reaction and tyranny fear no prophet but a living one."

" Surely," I questioned, " Jesus is the great exception? "

" He is the great example," Doubt sneered. " Jesus taught meekness and meekness is despised as a vice; he taught the superiority of the spiritual over the material world, and we have a society built on the assumption that might makes right; he taught love and the world is corroded with hate; and our admiration goes out to those who can make others serve them; he taught poverty, and the very church which he founded has grown rich on the fruit of sweat shops and prostitution. Only the other day a Bishop took up a paper and read that poem, which has been going the rounds of the press :

Said the Pacifist " He only killed my
    brother, and
  Resistance isn't right !
Said the Pacifist "He only kicked my
    mother,
  And its very wrong to fight !

I think its wicked rather, to defend
    An aged father, for it might end in a
        quarrel.
If a Hun assaults your sister (said the gentle
Pacifister), turn your other sister to him
And be moral.

He laughed gleefully. " That's a good joke
on Jesus," he said.   Then he put on his
bishop's garb and went forth to dedicate the
church of The Holy Saviour, the last instal-
ment of the debt having been paid off by two
great financiers as a thank-offering for the
defeat of a bill restricting child labour.

" So you see," concluded the Fiend, " there
is no immortality for ideas or ideals in
martyrdom. God sends his prophets to every
generation to translate into the language of
their time the few fundamental truths all great
men have thought since the beginning of the
world, and the story never varies—the world
receives them not."

So I wrestled through the night with Doubt,
until at last in the dawn I sat up and looked
him squarely in the face. "Very well," I
said, " suppose I serve only my own generation, I shall serve it with such light as God
has given me and, my time being a part of all
time, I shall have served humanity."

CHAPTER XXXV.

OUT OF JAIL.

After a week I was let out on bail, to be tried at the midsummer assizes. Some of my radical friends—Ned, of course—came to the jail to meet me, but I would not let them come home with me because I wanted to go alone to Colin. He had come to see me once in jail, but he had been very quiet and I was afraid I had lost his regard. I had not let him know when I would be released, because I thought I would rather talk things out with him alone.

It is not possible for me to do more than set down here the bare fact of Colin's seeming desertion, and that, though I had written to McNair some weeks before I actively engaged in Pacifist propaganda, and quite a long time before my arrest, I had had no word from him. True, I had freed him from our friendship for the duration of the war, as I was unwilling to compromise his position as an officer of the army, but I had not expected silence as the answer, and I had thought Colin loved me a little after the fashion in which

I loved him. It was difficult enough to bear
the reproaches of mother, who had gone to
California for her health, accompanied by
Jean, and of Jean herself, but for Colin and
McNair to fail me—that was my real cross.

It happened that on my way home to my
room I met Pauline. She looked the other
way, and I slunk past her apologetically, diffidently, and hated myself unspeakably for that
inward shrinking.

I walked on, repeating to myself those words
of Henley's so dearly loved by all cowards and
weaklings :

' It matters not how straight the gate,
' How charged with punishment the scroll.
' I am the master of my fate;
' I am the captain of my soul.' "

I found Colin watering the plants in my
room.

" Hello ! " I said, with bravado, for I was
afraid of Colin.

He looked up gravely. " Hello ! " he
exclaimed, in surprise. His face looked years
older.

I took off my hat, and began to fidget about
the room. Colin set down the pitcher and
came over and put his arm about my shoulders.

" I want you to talk to me about the war, little woman, and tell me why you feel as you do," he said.

" Come here, laddie," I replied, drawing him over to a chair. We sat down and Colin waited for me to begin, but I didn't begin. I leaned over and patted his hand.

" Colin," I said, " you're McNair's boy. I am not going to use my influence while he is away to turn you against the thing for which he stands, but you have a right to hear the other side. Read any of the radical magazines and books in my little library— "

" They've taken them all away," he interrupted.

" Then read your history and think, sonny. Or read what the editors are saying, and think. Or read the Bible and think. Or read nothing at all, if you like, but just think. Think of your own experience on the playground at school. Think whether it is not true that a soft answer turneth away wrath; whether love or vengeance is harder to resist."

Colin came and knelt beside my chair and put his arms about me and kissed me. " I have been thinking, little mother," he laughed, " until my cocoanut's aching."

I was so happy. It was the first time Colin had called me mother.

* * * * *

Mrs. Fleming had decided that I was not a desirable boarder, not being " for the Hempire," as she said; so I found a room in the home of a courageous young radical, with a family, who risked his position in taking me in.

That was three weeks ago, and to-day (May day, by the way) my heart is singing as it did that winter night, years ago, when I put my hand in McNair's and felt the thrill of his touch go up my arm and down into my heart.

For I've had a telegram from McNair, asking me to meet him at the station. I cannot meet him. I have promised to address a meeting at the market square at the time the train comes in, but I'll see him in a few hours; I'll feel the touch of his hands, and perhaps of his arms and his lips.

Oh, McNair, my heart is as light as thistle-down to-day! For all its stupid blundering, what a glorious old world it is !

If only I could meet you at the train. Why not? Why not get someone else to take my place at the meeting? And have them think they have succeeded in intimidating me? Yet it is only once in a lifetime that one's lover comes home from the war.

I'll do it. I can imagine the way you will step off the train, limping a little, and stop and look round, and I can picture the lighting up of your face as you see Colin and me.

If I go to the meeting they will probably arrest me and put me in jail again. And you just home! I'll not go. I cannot go. Surely that isn't necessary. But the whole point of the meeting is that it is to be addressed by one who has been in jail and who refuses to be silenced.

Oh McNair, why did you say that about coming out strong. I don't want to come out strong. I want to be weak and conventional. I want to be happy. Carlyle says : " What act of legislature was there that thou should'st be happy? " None. I do not need Carlyle to tell me that. Laid alongside the great tape measure of eternity the months I might spend in jail would be insignificant. I know that if I were to read the chapter on ghosts, which I am resolved not to do, that fact would emerge triumphant. But I know nothing of eternity. All I am sure of is the little space of time between my birth and death. It may be that

the light does not go out at the end, but passes
on clearer than ever to other spheres. It may
be that those Orientals are right who believe
that we are reabsorbed into some great con
sciousness. It may only be that we become
an undying part of the evolving consciousness
of our own world, that as I am the product
of all the lives that have preceded mine, so I
in turn will go to make a part of all the
lives that will come after me. That would be
immortality of a sort. But I think it is better
than that; a new chance perhaps, in a world
where our natural instincts will be less antagon-
istic to our ideals.

*   *   *   *   *

I have read the chapter on ghosts.
Obviously the postponement of our happiness
for a few months or years doesn't matter.
But when one looks at events in a big enough
way to make them shrink to tolerable pro-
portions the good one hopes to accomplish
shrinks also. Yet there is still left a tiny
residue of God-likeness in sacrifice. So I go
to the meeting.

CHAPTER XXXVI.

AFTER AN INTERLUDE.

Going through McNair's papers the other day I found this manuscript written by Aleta Dey ten years ago, worn and almost illegible in parts, for McNair had read and re-read it. My wife, looking over my shoulder, exclaimed, " What is that, Colin? "

" Read it, dear," I said, putting it into her hands. " I don't think the little woman would mind."

Some hours later she returned, laid it on my desk, and went away again without speaking. She did not refer to it until that evening when we were sitting out on the veranda of our little home overlooking English Bay and watching the clouds play about the peaks of the snow-capped mountains. Then she got up suddenly and came and stood behind my chair and slipped her arms about my neck and stammered : " Would you—would it be wrong —do you think we could publish that story? "

We talked it over for a long time and decided we might, with the conclusion of the sad little tale.

When McNair got off the train the night of
that day on which Aleta Dey made the last
entry in her autobiography he looked around
quickly, and, seeing me alone, he turned pale.
" The little woman? " he asked, anxiously.

I gave him the note she had sent, and he
read it, smiling.

" Let us go along to the meeting, laddie,"
he said, happily.

We went, and as we got down from the
street car we saw a howling mob gathered
around a small figure on a chair. It was Aleta
Dey. As we reached the edge of the crowd
someone struck her and she fell over backward. At that McNair gave a terrible cry and
began to fight his way to the heart of that
struggling, cursing mob, and I followed in the
path he opened.

I think the mob was a little stunned to see
this huge soldier rush up and gather the tiny
form in his arms and kiss the still white face.
" Little woman, speak," he moaned. " It's
McNair."

She lay like a stone in those strong arms in
which she had so longed to rest.

Someone touched him on the elbow. " The
doctor's come, sir."

McNair stood by, chewing his military

moustache fiercely during the examination. The doctor looked up and shook his head.

" Dead? " McNair asked, hoarsely.

" Not yet," the doctor answered.

McNair laid his hand heavily on my shoulder.

*   *   *   *   *

Aleta Dey lay on a white cot in a private ward of the hospital.   Death was creeping slowly up her body from the injured spine to the heart.

McNair sat leaning over the cot on one side, stroking her pretty hair.   From time to time he stopped to press his lips to hers, and he kept a firm hold of her little hand as if to draw her back from the unseen world into which she was slipping.

I sat on the other side of the cot, too miserable for words.   Aleta Dey was dying.   McNair was broken-hearted.   Nothing seemed worth while.

" It's nice to have you and Colin at hand," Aleta said, smiling at me.

McNair raised his head and looked at me coldly.   " Hasn't Colin been at hand all the time, dear? " he asked, quickly.

" You forget that I have been under lock

and key," she answered; " but of course Colin stood by."

McNair said nothing more, but I knew he was not satisfied. Silence fell upon the clean grey little room with the spotless cot and the green shaded light.

A nurse tip-toed in and out again, leaving us three alone once more.

A few intimate friends associated with her in her work had come, said their long farewell and gone away. Ned Grant had been last. When he entered the room McNair stooped and whispered something to Aleta, then he motioned to me to follow him into the hall.

" He loves her, laddie," he said, by way of explanation.

When Grant came out he approached McNair and held out his hand. " Thank you, Captain," he said, gravely. " I don't suppose we could ever be friends, but I understand why Aleta loves you."

McNair blushed like a boy, as he took Grant's hand and pressed it warmly. " I see no reason, sir, why we cannot be friends," he protested. " I shall always have a very warm regard for those who stood by her through this time.

" I'd be glad to—to—have your help later on," he added, as Grant turned away.

Grant nodded, and walked swiftly down the corridor.

So they left us alone with her. With faculties amazingly clear at first her mind turned constantly to the cause for which she had given her life.

" I have been brought into this world," she said once, "without any choice on my part, and have been given a mind, for which I did not stipulate, at variance with my time. Then the world says to me, ' You must stay in this world, for to take your own life is a crime, and you must agree with your time, or if you cannot agree you must make of your life one long hideous lie by pretending that you see eye to eye with your generation.'

" I tell you, McNair," Aleta's eyes blazed with their former fire and her voice rang with almost its old vigor, " the tenantry of no human body is of sufficient moment for a soul to submit to such an indignity as that. I am not sorry they have foreclosed my mortgage on this house of clay. At last I am unafraid— "

She coughed, turned restlessly and fell silent.

After a time she resumed where she had
left off, having apparently been turning it over
in her mind : " If there is anything on the
other side of death, and I believe there is, it
must be freedom. It must be that over there
there will not be a thousand souls with clubs
standing over one and daring him to tell the
truth as he sees it. Otherwise, pray God that
the thing that is a few hours ahead of me may
be annihilation."

McNair pressed her hand in wordless misery.

About midnight there came a gentle tap at
the door and Pauline came in. McNair
moved away and she fell on her knees at
Aleta's side and kissed her very tenderly. They
did not speak of the past. Perhaps it seemed
too trivial.

" Write to mother and Jean, Pauline,"
Aleta said, when Pauline was leaving, " and
tell them if they want to do something to
please me to be good to my boys."

" I'd like you to write to mother too, dear,"
she said to McNair, when Pauline had gone
out.   " She is ill in California partly on
account of me, and she and Jean may think
of me as having died alone among strangers.
I want them to know "—she looked up into
McNair's face with an expression of adoration

I shall never forget—" that—that I died in the arms of the greatest lover in the world."

And that was true.

* * * * *

Towards morning she spoke again : " Of this I am sure, as I stand at the door of death, or of life, that the only conquering force in the world is love. If I have failed to convince those with whom I have come in contact it is because I have preached love without living it."

" Don't," McNair said, stroking with a shaking hand the beautiful red brown hair; " I can't bear that."

Aleta laid her soft white little hand on his huge one with a gesture of infinite tenderness. " You must try not to mind so much about my going, dear," she urged. " Except for leaving you and Colin I'm—I'm glad to go. I've always been a coward."

Presently she gave a soft little laugh. " I borrow to be born a Tory or brave in the next life."

McNair caught his breath in a dry hard sob. " Aleta, my fearless little darling, please don't," he begged. " I can't stand to hear you talk like that."

She smiled at him wistfully and sank into a stupor.

Once again she stirred.

"Don't let any harm come to the boy who —did—it," she whispered. "He risked his life——fair that I should risk mine."

"Very well, dear," McNair answered, master of himself again. It was wonderful the way he kept up through that awful night.

Just as the dawn was creeping in about the drawn shades the light faded from her face, leaving it pale and still.

CHAPTER XXXVII.
McNair Gives Way.

McNair had sat in my room, his head bowed in his hands, ever since I had made him come away from the hospital. Nobody could rouse him. Mr. Grant came to ask about the funeral arrangements. McNair stared at him blankly. The question was repeated.

" Her favourite chapter of the Bible was the fortieth of Isaiah," he said. " Tell the preacher to read that at the service," and he relapsed into gloomy silence.

Grant waited, hoping he would say more.

In the meantime a returned soldier came in and approached McNair. " The boys of our regiment are feeling mean about one of our men having killed a woman. Some of us think it is poor business to go to France to fight for freedom and kill our women off for asking for it at home, no matter how wrong-headed they may be.

" And—and so, sir, they thought they would like to send our band to the funeral to clear the name of the regiment and out of respect to you, sir."

The bowed figure in the shabby khaki uniform did not stir, and I wondered if he had heard.

A stillness fell upon the room. The soldier cleared his throat.

"What shall I say, sir," he began again, shuffling from one foot to the other.

McNair was roused at last. "Don't talk to me of right or wrong," he said, bitterly; "I only know she was the woman I loved—— stood by me when I was down. She carried me up to God by her faith in me.

"And—and—now when I've come back to her—" he broke off and his great fists clenched and unclenched spasmodically—"she's gone and I am left alone.

"In the slime and mud of the trenches I used to dream of this coming back. I used to think how I'd care for her and protect her. She was such a wee thing—such a brave wee thing——and now this. She's gone—nothing ahead but a blank."

He fell into a dark brooding silence, as he glowered fiercely, with angry resentful eyes, at the smiling spring day.

The soldier touched him hesitatingly and respectfully on the arm. "About the band?" he suggested diffidently.

" Get out," McNair shouted sharply, roused
to sudden fury. " Don't any of you dare to
come near her dead body. Don't you dare."

Mr. Grant came forward from the shadow
of the window curtain. He was very pale.
" I think she would have liked it Captain,"
he said, quietly.

McNair's head drooped. All the fire and
fury left him at once. He turned his haggard,
deeply-furrowed face to the soldier. " Very
well," he said, in a voice of inexpressible sad-
ness, " let them come."

CHAPTER XXXVIII.

THE FUNERAL.

There is a grandeur in the Dead March in Saul at any time. Accompanied by a tragedy like that of Aleta Dey, which shocks a whole city into thoughtfulness, it is overwhelming.

McNair had elected to walk with me behind her coffin. "There won't be many to do her honour," he said; "let us do what we can. Unless," he added, a little coldly, "you would rather not."

"See here, McNair, what do you mean?" I asked, angrily.

"I think you know," he answered.

"I know you think I went back on Aleta when she was in prison, but I didn't, only I was worrying a lot because as I came near to military age I had to choose between her faith and yours, and I was pretty busy thinking."

"Was that it, my boy?" he asked, eagerly.

"McNair," I said, hotly, "what do you take me for? Didn't she give me the only mothering I ever had in my life?"

He pressed my arm affectionately.

So on the day of the funeral we walked
along the middle of the wide clean sunny street
side by side, and after us came many more.
McNair was wrong about there being few to
follow her. Her death brought hundreds of
people with Pacifist leanings, who had said
nothing about it, to declare themselves openly.
Others, I fancy, joined the procession to clean
the hands of the city of the death of a woman
who cared more for her principles than for
life or liberty. Perhaps because McNair was
the chief mourner no attempt was made by
Aleta's Pacifist friends to make it the occasion
of a demonstration, other than that the
ordinary hearse was discarded and the coffin
laid upon an open waggon draped in black.
It was banked with flowers, people from all
parts of the Dominion having paid her the last
tribute.

It was very awkward for the authorities that
Aleta's lover was a soldier. They were afraid
of the funeral, and afraid of stopping it.
I think now that they were also afraid
of the spirit of tolerance and real freedom McNair preached as he marched with
slow heavy step behind that coffin. I seemed

to sense a tension in the air as we wound
slowly along the street to the solemn throb of
the music.

The sound of the drum and bugle died away
at the graveside, and the preacher opened the
Bible and began to read. The first words that
caught my attention were :

> " The voice of him that crieth in the
> wilderness, Prepare ye the way of the
> Lord, make straight in the desert a high-
> way for our God."

There was a stirring in the crowd as the
words rang out like a challenge on the clear
spring air. Some were present who were not
prepared to admit that hers was a voice crying
in the wilderness.

The preacher read on :

> ———" The voice said ' Cry.' And he
> said ' What shall I cry? ' All flesh is
> grass, and the goodliness thereof is as the
> flower of the field."

Boy though I was, I remember thinking
" What's all the fuss about then if we pass like
the flowers of the field."

> " Who hath measured the waters in the
> hollow of his hand, and meted out heaven
> with the span, and comprehended the

dust of the earth in a measure, and weighed the mountains in scales, and the hills in a balance."

Imagine the effect of that picture of the immensity of God as we stood beside that yawning grave.

The solemn melodious sentences rolled on, like chords of a mighty pipe-organ :

" Behold the nations are as a drop of a bucket, and are counted as the small dust of the balance : behold he taketh up the isles as a very little thing.

" And Lebanon is not sufficient to burn, nor the beasts thereof sufficient for a burnt offering.

" All nations before him are as nothing ; and they are counted to him less than nothing and vanity."

I looked about me, with a new sense of the bigness of things, and I noticed that the tension in the faces of the listeners had relaxed. I am sure they saw, as I did, man's fierce little hates shrinking into insignificance as the Hebrew prophet continued to paint that tremendous picture of the impartiality of God.

" Have ye not known? have ye not heard? hath it not been told you from the beginning? have ye not understood from the foundations of the earth?

" It is he that sitteth upon the circle of the earth, and the inhabitants thereof are as grasshoppers; that stretcheth out the heavens as a curtain, and spreadeth them out as a tent to dwell in :

" That bringeth the princes to nothing; he maketh the judges of the earth as vanity."

I remembered having read in one of Aleta's articles, " Each little group of grasshoppers has had the impiety to conscript the God of the universe to be the mascot of its armies. He must laugh, if the divine pity were not as far beyond our understanding as the divine habit of thinking in thousands of years is beyond our childish way of imagining that our day is the one day God ever dreamed.

" Yea, they shall not be planted," rang out the voice of the preacher, " yea they shall not be sown : yea their stock shall not take root in the earth; and he shall blow upon them and they shall wither, and the whirlwind shall take them away as stubble."

I cannot describe the solemn grandeur of that service. Aleta Dey dead seemed to be more alive than ever. The peace of a new and better understanding settled upon our souls, and sent us away, for the time being at least, cleaner and kinder men and women.

CHAPTER XXXIX.

McNair Passes On.

McNair went home from Aleta Dey's funeral and went to bed. On learning that she might go to prison he had written her at once—a letter which was probably submarined. Then he set about getting his discharge from the hospital in order to come to her. He had not been really fit to travel, and the long journey, with the shock at the end, had proved too much for him. He seemed to lose his grip on life. I tried to coax him to make an effort to get better for my sake, but he would only answer, " You belong to another generation, Colin. You have your own life to make. I'm not afraid but that you'll make a good job of it for the little woman's sake. But she belonged to my time. I can't seem to get started again without her."

Ned Grant came to see him very often and was exceedingly kind. McNair would listen by the hour to stories of Aleta's childhood, which Grant never tired of telling.

Pauline Ransome and Aleta's mother and sister came and did everything they could to

soften those last days, but the only bitterness
I ever knew McNair to show was in his
inability to quite forgive Pauline and Jean
for having turned against Aleta, by whose
side in a month's time he was laid.

Years afterward my wife and I went out and
planted flowers on their graves—pansies on
hers and poppies on his, and when we went
back two summers later the pansies had crept
from her grave on to his and the poppies from
his grave on to hers. We looked at each
other and smiled. "In death they were not
divided," my wife quoted, softly.

*   *   *   *   *

Under McNair's pillow when he died was a
tattered letter. He used to read it over almost
every day, and sometimes, near the end, he
would say to me, "Colin laddie, will you
read it to me—the little woman's last letter."

This was it :

" Dear McNair,

" I ought to have written this letter weeks
ago, but my disinclination was so great I have
been trying to cauterize my conscience in this
direction. Now necessity leaves me no choice.

" I am obliged to give up your friendship
for the duration of the war, because I am

about to engage in active propaganda ques-
tioning the right of the government to spread
among the people of this country the disease
of silence, that loathsome cancer of the social
body, which breeds fear and suspicion and pre-
pares the soil for violence and scandals and
every conceivable form of evil thinking and
doing. I am satisfied that the great French
philosopher was right when he said : ' A
miasma exhales from crouching consciences,'
and I would avert this disaster from my
country if I could.

" Different as they seem to me it is almost
certain that the government will make no distinction between this protest and previous ones
I have made against the war, lumping them
all together as Pacifism, and the punishment
is imprisonment. It might not be well for
you to be known to be writing to a Pacifist
in jail, so I give you up—until after the war.

" I was deeply touched by your last letter
asking that I take you fully into my confidence
as to my reasons for opposing the war, and
particularly by your suggestion that my
reluctance was not very complimentary to
your cause.

" I know you think your faith would stand
the shock of such arguments as I could bring

to bear upon it. I think it might, too, but
the consensus of opinion on your side is so
overwhelmingly against us that I am afraid to
risk it.   Since the governments of all the
countries concerned in this conflict have
decided that with thousands of newspapers and
magazines trumpeting the case for war up and
down the land the faith of the people in their
cause would not survive the publication of the
most obscure Pacifist organ, I am not in a
position to contradict them, especially as they
have much information which the censor has
very unkindly denied to me.

" So I'll not give you any of the Pacifist
arguments, though, indeed, a cause whose
advocates instinctively decide that it can
answer its antagonists only with prison has
been so deeply censured by its friends that its
enemies are left speechless.

" Sooner or later that fact burns itself into
the intelligence, and that very tyranny becomes
an argument that is well-nigh irresistible.
There is no even half-evolved human mind
which really respects the bully's logic : ' I'll
lick you if you say that again.'

" I think they are mistaken, McNair.   I
believe if they allowed the most perfect freedom the majority of the people would still

choose war, for there is something in the
human heart which answers 'present' to the
roll call of force. All of us, militarist and
pacifist alike, have felt the impulse to kill the
thing we could not dominate.

"Perfect freedom of speech would make
just this difference : no little group of men
would be able to keep a country at war for
purposes which the majority of the people
disapproved. No, it would do more. It
would lift the cause of war to a new plane,
for we, all of us, in our heart of hearts know
that no group of men is sufficiently infallible
to be allowed to sift the truth for other men,
and we are at bottom deeply ashamed that
they should dare to try.

"If I wished for their punishment I should
stand aside and egg them on to bring about a
revolution by their tyranny, for the people
who will allow their consciences to be intimi-
dated are always dangerous people, and the
government which depends on their support
is playing with gunpowder.

"But I do not believe in revolution; I am
convinced that the only permanent conquest
is a spiritual one. And, moreover, there is
always the possibility that the war party is
right and I am wrong, and that if I had my

way the march of civilization would be
impeded. So I ask only this, that men be
given the whole truth. So far the government
has never told the people anything until they
found it out through the scullery—and then
grudgingly. Professing to be engaged in a
great crusade to make the world safe for
democracy they do not trust their own people
with any information which can possibly be
concealed from them. Do they imagine
Germany does not see the absurdity of this
position?

" The people are not swine looking for a
pleasant trough in the sun. Let them know
all the facts and they will choose the fine and
generous thing, whatever that may be. They
might choose your way, for I am not as sure
of the irresistible nature of my arguments as
is the government which would suppress them.
But in the full sunlight of truth people would
choose the good. This faith in my kind is the
one clear religion I have left; the only thing
which makes life tolerable in these hideous
days.

" I have told you this because I want you
to understand how impossible it is for me to
remain inactive any longer, though I should
like to do so for your sake.

" For I love you, McNair, and I think you know it, but I am putting it into words in case anything should happen to part us for all time. Life has been different for me ever since that night on the train when you turned to me with a twinkle in your eye and asked, ' Did I turn too soon? ' I believe I loved you instantly. Not as I love you now after our rich years of happiness, but as my mate, as the one man to whom I could surrender myself as a wife and the mother of children.

" Afterwards I learned to love you as a mother loves her child, generously and protectively as between you and me, selfishly and exclusively as between we two and the rest of the world.

" But at last, McNair, I've grown to love you with the highest form of human affection —I love you as my friend. I love you well enough to give you up for the ends of righteousness, which are greater than this human love of ours.

" It is so great a thing, this love of mine, that I have no shame in speaking of it. I think you love me just as I love you, but if I am wrong in this you will not, I am sure, feel that it binds you in any way, as a commoner man might do. You are too under-

standing to pity anyone for having loved, even
without love's logical fulfillment.

" Just after I had begun to love you I heard
some women talking about a woman friend
whose engagement had been broken off
because the man had learned to care for someone else. And they were sorry for the woman.
That seemed to me very strange. What sort
of meagre little loves must theirs have been
that they could pity anyone for having loved
as I love you, McNair?

" Perhaps they had never loved and did not
know what love does to one's life; that it is
a permanent mirage bringing into sight
unguessed landscapes in the realm of sympathy
and understanding. Nothing of change or
disappointment can take away from one this
new horizon.

" So I count it the crowning success of my
life that I have loved so good a man. It would
have been magnificent to have loved any man
as I love you, dear one, but to have loved
a man who is so much more than just a mate,
who has never cheapened my sincerity by
flippant word or look, who is the one I would
have chosen out of all the world to be my
friend — Life has been very generous to give

me this. Remembering that, I shall try not
to complain whatever lies ahead.

" I shall hear of you through Colin and
you of me, and daily—hourly almost—I shall
pray for your safety and happiness, my dear,
dear one.

" When it comes to a time like this, training
in writing helps one very little to reveal one's
heart. I don't know how to tell you what
I feel other than to say again I love you, and
leave you to guess the gestures and caresses
with which I would tell it you if you were
here. I love you so exactly as a dear old
Tory like you wants to be loved that I am
almost ashamed of myself; with so complete
a surrender of my womanhood to your man-
hood——

" I must not speak of that. Were I to
begin to think how much I want you here—
but that way lies weakness. Out of this love
of ours has come something bigger than
human love which I must not betray; something which has inspired both of us to do
greater things than either could have achieved
alone.

" I am sorry that to-day our causes seem
to stand in opposition; but perhaps it is only
seeming. It may be that history with its

wider perspective will discover them to be two branches of the same tree of freedom, yours contending with the winds of tyranny abroad and mine with the winds of tyranny at home.

" And if we should not meet again in earthly life, but should pass on to other spheres of action, we'll do great things together there, dear one, because we've gone through this content with the will for righteousness, and leaving each the other one to choose his path."

FINIS.

Other Canadian Novels of Interest

Margaret Laurence

THE STONE ANGEL
In this beautifully crafted novel, first published in 1964, Margaret Laurence explores the life of one woman, the irascible, fiercely proud Hagar Shipley. Now over ninety and approaching death, she retreats from the bitter squabbling of her son and his wife to reflect on her past— her marriage to tough-talking Bram Shipley ('we'd each married for those qualities we later found we couldn't bear'), her two sons, her failures, and the failure of others. Her thoughts evoke not only the rich pattern of her past experience but also the meaning of what it is to grow old and to come to terms with mortality.

Forthcoming Novels in the Manawaka Series

The Fire-Dwellers
The Diviners

Margaret Laurence

A JEST OF GOD

Rachel Cameron, thirty-four and unmarried, is trapped
by the stifling conventionality of small-town Canadian life
as a shy, retiring schoolmistress and dependable helpmeet
to her coy and overbearing invalid mother. Desperate for
love and companionship, she risks her all in an affair with a
man for whom sex and love are more trivial matters—and
it changes Rachel's life in unforeseen ways. First published
in 1966, this is the second of Margaret Laurence's famous
Manawaka series of novels, and a powerful exploration of
loneliness, desire and the pain of disappointment.

*Filmed as 'Rachel, Rachel', directed by Paul Newman and starring
Joanne Woodward*

Forthcoming Titles in the Manawaka Series

The Fire-Dwellers
The Diviners

Margaret Atwood

THE HANDMAID'S TALE

Offred is a national resource. In the Republic of Gilead her viable ovaries make her a precious commodity, and the state allows her only one function: to breed. As a Handmaid she carries no name except her Master's, for whose barren wife she must act as a surrogate. But Offred cannot help remembering subversive details of her former life: her mother, her lover, her child, her real name, women having jobs and being allowed to read, fun, 'freedom'. Dissenters are supposed to end up either at the Wall, where they are hanged, or in the Colonies, to die a lingering death from radiation sickness. But the irrepressible Moira shows Offred that it is possible to cheat the system . . .

'An unrepeatable and starkly individual performance'—
London Review of Books
Shortlisted for the Booker Prize for Fiction, 1986

Other Novels by Margaret Atwood

Bodily Harm
Dancing Girls
The Edible Woman
Lady Oracle
Life Before Man
Surfacing

AMERICAN MODERN CLASSICS

DOROTHY BAKER
Cassandra at the Wedding

JANE BOWLES
Two Serious Ladies

MARTHA GELLHORN
Liana
A Stricken Field

ELIZABETH HARDWICK
The Ghostly Lover
The Simple Truth
Sleepless Nights

ZORA NEALE HURSTON
Their Eyes Were Watching God

PAULE MARSHALL
Brown Girl, Brownstones

TILLIE OLSEN
Tell Me A Riddle
Yonnondio: From the Thirties

GRACE PALEY
Enormous Changes at the Last Minute
The Little Disturbances of Man

ANN PETRY
The Street

EUDORA WELTY
Delta Wedding
Losing Battles
The Optimist's Daughter
The Ponder Heart
The Robber Bridegroom

DOROTHY WEST
The Living Is Easy

ANZIA YEZIERSKA
Hungry Hearts and Other Stories